Praise for

Pearl Harbor

If you like to read about history in a way that makes you feel you're right there, if historical details fascinate you as much as the emotions of the people who were involved in those events, and if you love books with characters who are so life-like they make you think they are people you have met, you will love Abiding Heart as much as I did. I cannot wait for the next one! ~ *Queer Magazine Online*

Avenging Heart gives an accurate picture of the post-war rebuilding efforts in Honolulu (and Hawaii as a whole), but with characters who are so life-like they make you think they are people you have met, this is a treat for anyone. If you are interested, I do recommend starting with the first book—this series is simply wonderful and best read in sequence for the full effect... ~ *QMO Books*

Total-E-Bound Publishing books by A.J. Llewellyn:

Pearl Harbor Volume One
Vagabond Heart
Gypsy Heart

Anthologies:
Sins of Summer: Burnt Island
Sins of Autumn: Full
Sins of Winter: If Come
Sins of Spring: The Kaupe

The Mediator
The Bouncer
Paper Valentine
Stavros

PEARL HARBOR
Volume Two

Abiding Heart

Avenging Heart

A.J. LLEWELLYN

Pearl Harbor Volume Two
ISBN # 978-1-78184-501-1
©Copyright A.J. Llewellyn 2012
Cover Art by April Martinez ©Copyright November 2012
Interior text design by Claire Siemaszkiewicz
Total-E-Bound Publishing

Published in 2010 by Total-E-Bound Publishing, Think Tank, Ruston Way, Lincoln, LN6 7FL, United Kingdom.

ABIDING HEART

Dedication

I dedicate this book to all the POWs, those still living
and those in repose.

Author's Note

I would like to thank all the people who reached out to me when Vagabond Heart and Gypsy Heart were published, sharing stories of their own families' experiences at Pearl Harbor. I have been touched to learn of their lives during the events of that fateful day, and in the aftermath of the attack on December 7, 1941.

My thanks to Linda Lang, who shared her father's wartime correspondence with me. His unsent letters, depicting a young man's fears, really touched my heart.

In life, he never discussed what happened to him as a POW in Japan, Korea and China. The discovery of his missives — wedged in an old travel guide—in the year since his passing, is his painful legacy that his children are only now beginning to understand.

Like many POWs he had never come to grips with what happened to him, yet could not find the words to convey his feelings to those around him.

I would like to thank my awesome WWII expert Merrylee Lanehart, for combing over each and every page of this series for accuracy.

My biggest thanks go to my amazing editor, Stacey Birkel, who has worked so diligently on these stories and Abiding Heart, the third chapter of Tinder and Jason's love story.

And, finally, my thanks to Dee Wyeth who came up with the title for this book.

~A.J. Llewellyn

Chapter One

Honolulu, Hawaii
Wednesday, January 21, 1942

I lay in bed, listening for my lover's footfall. It was a little before seven o'clock in the morning and he'd been gone almost an hour. I wrestled with my desire to give him a little more time before I charged off looking for him. I let out a breath. I hadn't been aware that I'd been holding it, not really, but I worried each time he was away from me. I never said anything, but I felt my fears were reasonable considering that he had been captured by Japanese forces at sea just a few short weeks ago.

Miraculously, he'd managed to escape.

I kept giving myself reasons to stay in bed, keeping it warm for him, just like he'd asked me to. I held the pillow that contained his scent — ylang ylang and sandalwood. I gave myself up to the sweet, soothing sounds of The Andrews Sisters singing *I'll Be With You In Apple Blossom Time*. I wanted to be with Jason all the time. I entertained myself by imagining what I would do to him when he came home.

The lush, yet breezy harmonies relaxed me. I had almost drifted off when my lover, who'd had a rough night's sleep, walked back into our little Chinatown studio.

He gazed at me the way he always did lately, as though he couldn't believe he was with me, that I was real. I saw the emotions crossing his face as I smiled, holding my arms out to him. He dropped his gas mask on the bedside table. The music stopped and the radio announcer read off the latest news bulletin.

"All citizens be alert. There will be fines issued to anyone seen without their gas masks—"

"Turn it off, baby, please," Jason begged.

Music was fine. Constant, negative news was hard to take, especially when war bulletins came in each and every minute. I understood how he felt. He was weary. Bone weary. I was his respite.

I leaned over my side of the bed.

"Let me find some music," I said. I fiddled with the dials. We'd picked up the astounding 1937 Deforest Crosley tube radio and twenty-three-inch tall cabinet for the princely sum of three dollars at one of the many yard sales that had sprung up around the islands over the last few weeks. With families leaving Hawaii in droves, they were desperate to offload the things they thought they couldn't ship back to the mainland. It was in immaculate condition and the sound quality was superb. We liked to turn the radio's 'magic eye' and find our favourite music as we lay in bed. We adored making love to Glenn Miller, Artie Shaw and The Andrews Sisters. For the minutes we listened to their lovely songs, the world was a beautiful, peaceful place again…

We had a fully furnished home in Waikiki, but I had turned it over to the military government as a gesture of goodwill whilst my lover had been on a clandestine mission for our country. Jason still hadn't quite forgiven me, but I had taken out some of his favourite antiques, his clothes, books — and a box of booze — so we had everything we needed.

I so loved the little studio he owned in a back alley off Maunakea Avenue. We'd managed to pick up some wonderful pieces of furniture and kitchen utensils for it. Jason liked to joke that we could hardly move because we had so much stuff, but I found it hard to walk past these frantic families without purchasing *something*. I loved that our new little home was big enough just for the two of us. And I loved living in Chinatown. In the months before he met me, the studio had been Jason's little crash pad. When he worked late at his bank, he would spend a few hours here then return to work. Now it was our love nest. Chinatown was our world. People accepted us…no, they embraced us.

No music. Just news. And none of it good.

"Turn it off, baby, I want to concentrate on you."

This time I did as he asked. I turned back to him. He had a lustful gleam in his eye as he kicked off his shoes, then dropped his trousers and shirt on the floor. As usual I got a thrill seeing him naked.

"Get in here, you." I held out my arms again and he slipped back under the covers with me. He smelt faintly of dry cleaner fluid.

A whole week we'd been back in Waikiki, and we'd thrown ourselves into our new projects. Jason had resumed running his family's bank here in Chinatown. He'd given loans to several local businessmen to take over stores that had been abandoned by people anxious to leave the islands, thanks to the attack on Pearl Harbor.

Jason himself had purchased two laundries and a dry cleaner. Together, we had given several friends money in order to plant and harvest fruit and vegetables at their homes—Victory Gardens that had started cropping up on the expansive windward side of the island to combat chronic food shortages.

Hopeful families in Waikiki had started planting in allotted spaces in public parks, and we had given them money, too. We hoped this positive war effort would be the antidote to the drunken, debauched honky-tonk bars that sold lethal imitation gin and watered-down drinks to the armed forces streaming into the islands.

He had left our bed at the crack of dawn to open all three of his businesses. He would return in a couple of hours to keep an eye on things. Restaurants, laundries and dry cleaners were the unexpected boom industries, thanks to the war effort. But right now, my job was Jason.

He snuggled in my arms, pressing kisses on my throat and neck. His cock fell against my warm thigh. Hmmm…it needed some attention. He moved his face up to kiss me.

"I love you," he said. I loved hearing it. I never got tired of hearing it, but I worried that he still hadn't told me what had happened to him out in the ocean when the Japanese forces seized his ship. Jason was understandably traumatised, but if he couldn't tell me, then how in the world was he going to tell the military tribunal next week?

My hands moved down his body. He shivered as the back of my hand grazed his leaking cock head. He was the most responsive lover I'd ever had. He lay back on his pillow and grabbed my head, threading his long fingers through my blond hair.

"Oh, Tinder." Our lips met, our tongues dancing against one another. My arm brushed against his cock. I wanted to suck it. As far as I was concerned only two things should ever touch his cock. My mouth and my ass.

He wouldn't let go of me. Sometimes—and this was only since we'd returned to Waikiki from rural Maui, when he had bad dreams and then plunged into the world of strangers—he seemed afraid. He never expressed this to me. It was just my feeling. As I kissed him, allowing my mouth to linger over his chin and down his throat, I decided that from now on, no matter what he said, I would accompany him wherever he had to go. My name came to his lips again as I licked a trail down his skinny chest. I loved every inch of his body. And he knew it.

"Please," he whimpered. "*Please.*"

I moved quickly to gobble up his cock head. His ass reached up to me at the much-needed contact. I got between his lovely thighs and began licking his balls. I'd discovered very early on in our relationship that Jason loved for me to suck them. They were surprisingly big, and for me they were always full. I tugged on the sac with my lips. He moaned. I let my tongue lave the balls beneath the skin, sucking them one at a time. I took a deep breath then got them both into my mouth.

Glancing up, I saw his slow, ecstatic smile transforming his worried face. I reached up and lightly stroked his cock at the base of his shaft. He was already erect and ready to go, but I hadn't finished with him yet.

I released his balls and went back to teasing the ball sac. I lifted his legs and he whimpered when my tongue went straight to his ass hole. He flopped around on the bed like a fish out of water as I jabbed my tongue into him.

"On your knees," I commanded. He didn't seem to be able to do it. He stared down at me in mute desire. I moved my face away from him, flipped him over and slapped his butt cheek. He got to his knees. I stuck my face right into his ass and began to suck him with renewed force. Resting on his elbows, he kept pushing back into my face. I reached around to touch his cock and felt its moisture at my fingertips. I hunched back, turned over and slid underneath him.

He let out a cry as my mouth reached his cock. I opened my lips and began to caress his sweet cock head. He worked hard to get his cock past my lips. I caved in to his mounting pressure and I felt his legs trembling on either side of my head as he began to fuck my mouth.

I relaxed, knowing this was one of Jason's favourite things to do, but he always worried about choking me. I wanted him to let it rip and give it to me. I slid my hands along his thighs and that seemed to do the trick. As I sucked and swallowed his meaty cock, he fucked me with a more determined pace.

Reaching one hand up to his slick ass, I slipped a finger inside him.

"*Gāocháo!*" he shrieked. "*Gāocháo!* I am coming!" He went off like a rocket, straight down my throat.

He didn't stop fucking my face and I didn't want him to. I'd moved a second finger inside him and he was still going crazy. I felt his cock softening just a little. He slowed down, rising on one arm to stroke my face and hair. I knew that if I gave him a few minutes, he would be ready for action again, but he rolled himself off me, my fingers slipping out of him.

Jason lay on his side, his face close to mine, staring at me. His eyes glistened with unshed tears.

"How did I ever think I could go off on a mission without you?"

I kissed his beautiful thick black eyebrows, teasing away the frowns with my insistent lips. My mouth roamed his face, his eyes gently closing under my chin.

"Temporary insanity?" I asked, moving away again.

Eyes still shut, he smiled.

"I don't know what you were thinking, mister, but just don't get any funny ideas about trying it again."

His brown eyes opened, his serious gaze meeting mine. "Don't worry, I won't."

Things were so intense between us. He looked away first, wiping at the tears that threatened to fall. He glanced back at me. "Think there might be some music on?"

"Let me check."

He fondled my ass as I leaned across the bed. Nope. Another bulletin. The same message about gas masks. The masks had been a novelty at first — now they were a nuisance. They were heavy and it was easy to forget them when you went from one place to another. All of us who had experienced the attack on Pearl Harbor understood that the masks were for our own good in case of another Japanese attack — there had been rumours of a possible poison gas attack — but it was difficult to watch little children lugging them along on the street. They should have been in school — running, jumping, singing songs. Instead, the schools were still closed and our island children stood with their exhausted, worried parents, lining up for everything from food to clothes.

Rumours had everyone jumpy – so jumpy the government started issuing news bulletins that all rumours should be squashed. They were afraid of even more residents stampeding towards the shipping terminals that were already overwhelmed with people desperate to leave the islands.

"Turn it off," Jason said, but he didn't seem upset. We'd listened for weeks for news of the captured crew of the SS *Malama* – the Matson cargo ship he'd been on when it was attacked. We'd scoured the newspapers and even asked my father, who'd resumed his work as the shipping officer for Liberty House department store, to make discreet enquiries about the fate of the captured prisoners.

There had been no mention of the ship's fate, but the newspapers had started to report on the Japanese attack on Hong Kong. They called it the Christmas Day Massacre and we'd been devastated to read the stories of what had happened to the people of the once-peaceful island after the defeat of the British, Canadian and Indian troops. Flushed with victory, the Japanese had executed fifty-three prisoners at Eucliff, beheaded them and rolled their bodies down the cliffs into the sea.

These stories began to alarm us islanders. Every day there seemed to be a new and increasingly atrocious story attached to the Japanese invaders.

I had no idea what exactly had happened to Jason, but I knew that he sometimes lapsed into silence, staring into space. I knew sex was good for him, but work was great.

"Let's get ready," I suggested.

He must have fallen asleep, because his eyes stayed closed and he didn't respond. I called it love therapy and happily let him rest some more. He'd awakened many times in the middle of the night. We'd had yet another practice air raid and this one had frightened him.

I started planning our day. I knew that keeping busy helped him deal with his demons. He'd thrown himself into the prospect of helping to rebuild Honolulu's businesses and I had been his strongest supporter every step of the way.

And then the letter had arrived from the war office just a few blocks away. Jason was required to give testimony about the attack on the SS *Malama*. He said he could do it and that he would, but I could see he was nervous whenever we talked about it.

I had rescued him and two other men with the help of a fisherman who took me to the island of Kaho'olawe. My presence was also required at the tribunal. I had asked my father to join us, and so far he was mulling things over. I would have been angrier with him had I not realised he was scared. The military government saw conspiracies and disloyalty *everywhere*, even when there were none. He would, I was sure, come around...but really, I had no idea if he would.

Just as I found a station playing some music, Jason reached out for me. "Tinder, you're too far away from me."

I rolled back towards him and moved into his arms. He began to hum to the Harry James song, *You Made Me Love You*.

"You did, you know—you made me love you." Jason kissed my eyes and forehead. I smiled into his shoulder. I knew we'd have to get up soon and I didn't want to. I ran my hands over his body, his beautiful cock stirring to life again under my touch.

I longed to ask him what had happened. I wanted to help ease his pain. Jason wrapped his arms around me and I fought off the wave of anguish I felt. I knew, in that moment, something terrible had happened and I wanted to die.

What the hell did they do to my man?

* * * *

He wanted to pleasure me, but I suggested we come home for a little…nooky…later. He loved that. We promised each other we'd come back home for lunch, but we had business to attend to. I would be with him all day, thank God, which eased my anxieties. We bathed together and dressed in our usual island attire of duck pants and Aloha shirts. Jason always went for subdued two-toned shirts. I went for bold colours. We slurped down coffee, eating big, sweet oranges over the kitchen sink. Jason kissed the juices from my chin and we left the little studio to face the big, mad world. He touched my hand briefly, his fingers curling into mine for just a moment, and then he handed me my gas mask. It was the third one I'd received. Since I was a repeat offender at losing mine, this latest replacement had cost me three dollars and fifty cents. I was determined to keep a better grip on this one.

Jason and I greeted all those we saw. Our little neighbourhood encompassed only several blocks but was the most heavily populated area of the whole island of Oahu. It was the first point of arrival for soldiers coming to the islands. Most never left the area. In fact, they were discouraged from doing so by the military. New military police patrolled the neighbourhood, and the prostitutes of Hotel Street had been rounded up after a brief period of freedom and were back to working the hotels.

There had been some controversy when a few of the working girls had raised their prices from the customary three dollars for three minutes. The police chief, Gabrielson—who really didn't want the vice in Chinatown—tried to have all the girls shipped off the island. In a public showdown with the military, the girls were allowed to stay. Executive Order 83 had been created by Gabrielson, who then leaked it to the *Honolulu Star-Bulletin*. Rumour had it that he wanted to embarrass the military for controlling prostitutes but it had backfired.

Now that the girls were fully under military control, they no longer feared police beatings and didn't have to pay the vice squad protection money. But it also meant that they were forced to regulate their price at three dollars a trick.

None of the uniformed men who lined Hotel Street waiting to 'climb the stairs' knew or cared anything about the drama. Fresh off their warships for anything from a day up to a week, they wanted to get laid, get drunk and get a tattoo. And not necessarily in that order.

At just nine in the morning, the lines had begun to form and the imitation gin that kept the soldiers drunk and happy was already flowing. We stopped by the dry cleaners. The widowed Mrs Wu—who had taken over the business from her brother and husband, both killed in the Pearl Harbor attack—rushed around her counter to hug us. My man had helped her and her sister-in-law with a loan and the business seemed to be running smoothly.

New laws had been passed by the military that there was to be a strict limit on available cash for all Hawaiians. Businesses could carry a float of five hundred dollars. Private citizens were allowed two hundred each. It was a crazy law that confused and frightened people. Mrs Wu asked Jason in her mixture of halting English and a few words of rapid fire Chinese what she should do if she found she had more than five hundred dollars in her shop.

He responded in English, since it was the law of the land now. "You should bank it," he said. "I am happy to help you." She seemed relieved. As we left she held her hands together as if in prayer and bowed to us in the traditional Buddhist way. We did the same to her.

"Where do you want to go next?" I asked him. "The laundries?"

He nodded. He seemed preoccupied.

"What's wrong, Jason?" I had to yell for him to hear me over the noise and chaos of Chinatown.

"Do you think there's another Tinder McCartney servicing the gay troops on Hotel Street?"

I tried not to feel hurt. I hated when he brought up my past. I'd been a prostitute for such a short time and he'd been my favourite client. He'd acknowledged many times that he would never have dated me had we met socially. He'd been deeply closeted when we met and had only had sex with male hookers—yet, from time to time he made mention of my past.

"Tinder," he said, "I am so jealous of every man you were with before me."

I relaxed. "Jason, I never loved anyone the way I love you."

"Not even Lauro?"

"Of course not. If I really loved him, I never would have tricked."

There, it was out. I'd always thought I'd loved Lauro, but I realised now it was nothing like the way I felt for Jason. He rocked on his heels, a sign he was pleased.

We walked to his bank, past the Buddhist temple, remarkably devoid of soldiers. Guess they didn't want to pray—only fuck. We retraced our steps, as we always did. We walked inside and gave a few dollars to the three monks who stood to receive any welcome strangers. Times were as tough for them as everybody else. They waved sticks of lit incense over us and banged the gong. I thanked them. I'd take my blessings any way I could get them.

As we walked down the street, we cut through the marketplace where uniformed men lolled around eating cheap bowls of soup and slurping down Five Island Gin shots. We often stopped to pick up something quick to eat.

One of the old Chinese stall holders beckoned to us from behind a row of cooked chickens dangling from meat hooks. We followed the slow-stepping grandma through the maze of hot stoves and leaking sinks. Steam rose in thick puffs around us. God, it made me hungry.

"Somebody you know is in trouble," she said. She pushed back wisps of grey hair from her face with gnarled fingers. Her troubled eyes were on my face, not Jason's.

"A friend of mine?" My hunger evaporated. I couldn't imagine who she was talking about. Lauro? No. The last I heard he was with his family in the Philippines, suffering from blindness due to the ravages of untreated gonorrhoea. At the tail end of our relationship, I had virtually kidnapped him and taken him to the hospital. The wonderful staff had saved his life and relieved him of most of the symptoms from his long-hidden illness.

"Melody," she said.

"Melody?" It took me a moment to sort through the names of people I knew from before the war and since I'd been a 'working man'. Melody. I was shocked. She had been a prostitute in the same hotel brothel as me. We'd befriended each other. As far as I knew, she'd gone back to the mainland, pregnant.

"Didn't she go back to San Francisco?" I asked.

Jason's head went from me to the old woman.

"She came back. She was working with Milaina again. I look after baby for her."

"Baby?" Jason's voice came out in a near shout. He began to question the woman in Chinese as I kept scanning the market, on the lookout for military officers who might take offence at his lapse in language.

Jason nudged me.

"Melody got beat up bad by the police. She hasn't been to see the baby for two weeks. Mrs Chan is worried. He's only a few months old. Melody was coming every day to breastfeed him. Since the beating, she's been to see him once. She came in a car with a military official." He continued to listen to the old lady as she dropped her voice and spoke in even faster Chinese to Jason. He looked mortified. He turned to me.

"The baby is sick. He has a bad cough. She has tried many remedies but Melody told her she couldn't take the baby to a doctor. She…" He seemed so upset now. "She says the baby has a fever. Mrs Chan hasn't heard from Melody since she came here all busted up." He let out a breath. "Melody has been working out of a house in Waikiki." He asked a few more questions.

He swivelled his gaze to me. "Guess who she's been tricking with?"

I had a pretty good idea. "Jean O'Hara?"

"You've got it. She bought a house near Black Point. The neighbours complained and she moved out. Now she's on a street right near the beach at Waikiki."

I groaned. That was exactly what Jean O'Hara would do. Jean was her own worst enemy. If she would only keep a low profile, she might not be the frequent target of police assaults. For a moment I could only feel utter amazement at the astonishing number of tricks she must have turned to have enough money to buy a house in Waikiki. I couldn't believe the way she flouted the rules by which the working girls were governed. There had been such strict conditions placed on them before Pearl Harbor, one of them being that they were not allowed to go near Waikiki Beach. She just *had* to go and buy a house there.

"It's another big, pretty house," Jason said. "I have to say—Jean is so clever. She buys houses, tells the neighbours she's going to open a brothel and they buy her out for more than she paid for it. That's a nice way to make a profit."

"We have to go there. Where is this house?" I was very worried now. Melody had left the island so she could keep her baby. What the hell had induced her to return? *Money.* It sickened me to know that she had tried to protect her child from her working life. I knew instinctively something awful must have happened for her to stay away from her helpless infant for two whole weeks.

"Mrs Chan doesn't know the address. She's only been there once but she said it's a blue house on Prince Edward Street."

We stood, both of us alone with our thoughts.

"What are we going to do with the baby?" Jason asked. "We can't keep him and if he's sick, he needs help."

I knew we had to take the child. No matter what.

"Where is he?" I asked.

The old lady certainly understood that okay. She pointed across the square. We followed her directions.

"His name is Christopher," Jason said. We knocked on the door of the old shoe store, just like Mrs Chan told us.

The middle-aged woman who greeted us seemed relieved. She took us past several stacked rows of shoe boxes to a hot kitchen where the sudden blast of a baby's wails pierced our ears.

Jason picked up the swaddled infant. I picked up his bags of belongings and the woman shooed us out like flies. In the square, the baby screamed and Jason slipped his pinkie finger into his mouth.

"I want to keep him," he said.

Oh, God. "We can't keep him. How do we explain him to people?"

"He's so helpless. I can't bear to think of somebody hurting him, Tinder."

This was so unlike Jason. "Let's take him home."

We raced across the market square, cutting back on to Maunakea and into the top of our alley, then ran to our studio. The baby's squalls were pitiful. Our neighbours were all working class families who were only home in the evenings. We put the baby on our bed and Jason opened up his damp, stained blanket and clothes as I hunted through his meagre belongings. There was a container of Johnson & Johnson's baby powder, some clean clothes and that was all.

"What were they feeding him? Anything there for a rash?" Jason asked.

"No. Nothing." I felt so bad for Christopher. He had a terrible rash.

He stared at us through a river of tears.

"We should put him in a cool bath." Jason picked up the baby, whose diaper was sodden. His poop looked green.

"Is that normal?" he asked me.

"How should I know? Jason…we need to get him to the hospital."

"No. I know a doctor. He'll help us." My lover sounded desperate. "Run a cool bath for me, please, Tinder."

I ran lukewarm water into the kitchen sink. He plopped the baby into it, holding him with such tenderness that my heart melted. The baby grinned through his terrible fever at the sensation of the cool water. Suddenly, I would have done anything I could to help him.

"Jason, I'm going to get him soap and some milk and…and…" I couldn't think.

"No. We're in this together." Jason's eyes glittered in anger. "I don't want anything to happen to you. Or to him." He looked at me. "We'll go together."

"Jason. He needs help. *Now*."

He sighed. "Call this number."

I ran to the phone and dialled the number. A male voice said, "Hello?"

"I am calling for Mr Jason Qui," I said.

"Do I hear a baby crying?" the man asked.

"Yes. My sister's baby is with us. He has a bad rash and…and…we've run out of formula."

"Formula? You can only get that by prescription now."

Jason kept telling me what to say.

"Yes," I repeated. On Jason's nod, I added, "And we are willing to pay."

A pause. "Where are you?"

I gave him the address and we waited.

Chapter Two

Dr Dao-Ming came into our home, looking startled at the packed furniture and lifting a brow at the cacophony coming from the kitchen.

"Somebody is most unhappy," he said. He was a middle-aged man with black hair, salt and pepper touching his temples.

In the kitchen, he took hold of the sobbing baby who was in Jason's arms. With a practiced air, the doctor shouldered the child, flipped open his black bag and withdrew a container of Similac.

"I have three of my own," he said, when he caught my awed expression.

He pointed to a baby bottle and instructed Jason how to prepare the formula. Jason measured the powder and added water and mixed it in the bottle. When the doctor turned Christopher over, the amateur theatrics stopped. He guzzled the formula until the doctor put the bottle down, then turned the baby onto his shoulder again and began to pat and stroke his back.

The doctor paced and eventually the baby burped. He resumed feeding him.

"He has a slight fever," he said after he checked the baby with a rectal thermometer, "but if you keep him cool and quiet, he should be okay."

Cool and quiet? We were two gay men living in the heart of Chinatown—the busiest, noisiest district on the island.

He shook the thermometer and dropped it into a glass container with liquid in it. "You can have this. Keep checking him every few hours, but he might just be hot. If he's been wearing all that wool right next to his skin, that explains the rash and his temperature. It's the worst kind of fabric for a tropical climate."

I had no idea how to respond. We'd only just taken over the baby's care. Now that we had the doctor here, however, I wanted to do everything I could for Christopher.

"What about the green poop? Is that normal?" I asked.

"How long has he been on formula?" he asked.

"Probably…a couple of weeks." That seemed the safest answer.

The doctor nodded. "Then that is quite normal." He frowned. "Unless his mother has been trying to dry-feed him."

Jason and I exchanged looks.

"I—we…don't know what dry-feeding is," I admitted.

"Have you been trying to feed him actual food?"

"Of course not," I said. *Oh, boy…had Mrs Chan?*

The doctor seemed relieved. "I know it's been a temptation with many a young mother in the islands now that certain foods are so hard to come by." The doctor scratched his chin. "I probably shouldn't say this, but the present government tried to make Similac hard for new mothers to get…as a way to urge them off the island."

I was stunned. What had happened to the Hawaii I knew? What had happened to aloha – to love, to sharing, caring…and, for God's sake, taking care of babies?

"What do we do then?" Jason asked.

"You have enough formula for a few days. You know where I am. I am happy to sell it to the child's mother whenever she needs it. For now, I would say the rash is his biggest problem. Judging by the condition of his diaper, he hasn't been changed for a while." I cringed under his accusatory glare. "He needs to be changed constantly."

"We understand," Jason said, in his best, client-coaxing tone. "We'll make sure he is."

The doctor smoothed some cream from a tube onto the baby's crotch.

"Do you have a fresh diaper?" he asked.

We had none. Jason shook his head. "Don't worry. We'll get some."

"Whose child did you say this is?" the doctor asked, looking from me to Jason.

"My sister," I said, since this was the lie we'd chosen to tell.

"And she is…where?"

"Working."

His expression changed. I could see a flash of sympathy for a new mother forced to go to work. "I see. So you're just helping out." He packed up his bag. "I'll leave you the tube. I noticed you have talcum powder. That will help keep him dry."

Jason followed him to the door and handed him a wad of cash. When we were sure the doctor had gone, Jason came over to me.

"Let's go, baby," he said.

I put a top on the baby and wrapped him in a small yellow, crocheted blanket, the only other clean one we had. Jason dropped the dirty baby things on the bathroom floor. As we walked down the alley, we made a checklist of things we needed.

We passed by Wo Fat's. Overnight, huge posters had been tacked to its exterior walls. *We Cook Up Anything But Rumours!* Every café and restaurant, even the bars now, had similar signs. It was sad that people were afraid that any comment could be misconstrued and used against them. And this was the response...

As always, we went to Yuen Yuen Company Limited, a gigantic store where you could buy just about anything...well, you could until the bombs dropped.

It was almost heart-breaking to see the meagre supplies of things. People still walked the aisles, though, looking for bargains. It felt almost surreal to find ourselves in the baby section. We bought diapers, a couple of packages of diaper pins, three baby bottles, a couple of soft blankets and two all-in-one jump suits that the sales assistant assured us would fit the baby.

We would have bought more, except we'd cleaned them out. As usually happened when we were in there, the staff plied us with a ton of other things...only in this case, we were grateful because they handed us a tube of the same cream the doctor had used on the baby, several bars of Fairy soap, a pair of pyjamas and some tiny infant socks.

We paid up, went back to the studio and cleaned our little buddy after he peed all over himself. We bathed him again using the soft-smelling, white baby soap. He seemed to love that. We put on a fresh diaper and, after we mastered the tight openings on the safety pins, put on his little jump suit. He started to wail.

"You think he's hungry again?" I asked.

Jason grinned. "How should I know? I know I am." His hand brushed against my cock, making me smile. He went to the kitchen and prepared a new bottle. We were both exhausted by the time we left the studio and ventured into the streets again.

"How do parents do this all the time?" I asked. We'd had to change Christopher's diaper and his clothes...twice. We'd thought we were all set for clothes and diapers and yet we'd romped through several things already. We left his soiled clothes and blankets at one of Jason's laundries. The women all tittered when they saw us walking in with a baby. Christopher, however, was as good as gold. He slept in Jason's arms. Poor little guy was as exhausted as we were.

We walked determinedly to the bank. Jason carried the baby. I carried our gas masks and a bag containing fresh diapers, rash cream and a bottle with Christopher's formula. I wasn't sure if the baby was supposed to have his own gas mask, but from what I'd seen there were no children's sizes and the ones we had would be far too big. Still, I worried that a military officer might stop and ask us questions.

All of Jason's counter tellers had been men before the war and he had made the decision to train women for the job now that so many of his male workers had either left the island or gone to work for the government. Jason liked to work with women, saying they were very detail-orientated.

A couple of them had huge crushes on him and it drove me crazy. He, however, never seemed to notice. One girl in particular — Jiao — always followed him around. In the days before he fell in love with me, she was exactly the sort of girl he would have kept around as his beard. In fact, one of our earliest dates had been a double disaster for me. He had not only forced me to partner up with a woman but had expected me to help him choose a wife.

Jiao was willowy and beautiful — the ambitious daughter of local, Chinese-born residents. I knew she had her heart set on Jason but, since his return from capture, he barely masked his annoyance when she fawned over him. I was surprised when Jason refused to let her hold the baby.

"He's fussy," Jason told her.

In his office, he raced through all the items in his in-box — a bamboo tray we'd found at one of the many yard sales we'd visited. He seemed to love that thing. He frequently touched it and stroked its intricate patterns. He held the baby with one arm and flicked through pages with the other.

I stood beside him, like a front-row sentry. There was nowhere for me to sit. All of his other office chairs were gone. He'd left the bank in the care of two trusted employees when he'd gone on his secret mission and they had stripped his office of everything — right down to its treasured antiques. When he unexpectedly returned, they were both embarrassed but explained his missing belongings.

We had found a new desk, a wonderful chair and the bamboo tray at a yard sale. I was determined to find more things for his office in the coming weeks.

He looked up, apparently surprised to see Jiao still standing there.

"I've signed everything," he said. "Was there something else?"

"My parents are having a cocktail party tomorrow night…well, evening…at the Royal Hawaiian Hotel right after the first aid classes. It will be over by curfew. I would love for you to be there. I…er, I think it would be good for business."

"I would like that, Jiao, but Timber and I have both had extensive first aid training and I have another commitment. I'm having dinner with Tinder and his father. As you know, he has been asked by the government to resume his duties as shipping officer for Liberty House. Helping him in the smooth, safe operation of importing goods from the mainland is, I think, also good for business."

He gazed down at the sleeping baby in his arms. Jiao opened her mouth, evidently thought better of it, then excused herself. She left with a venomous glance in my direction. I smiled sweetly back.

She closed the door behind her.

"That woman better watch how she treats you," Jason said, his voice low. "I won't tolerate anyone being rude to you."

I bent down and kissed him. He kissed me back heartily. Both of his employees who had taken over the day-to-day operations had quit when Jason returned. They saw his presence as a demotion. I knew Jiao wanted to be his second-in-command, but I also knew my lover didn't want to give her the position.

"We need a baby carriage," Jason said. "My arms are getting tired."

"He'll cry."

"No, he won't."

He handed the baby off to me. Ten seconds later, I'd had all the screaming I could handle for one day and passed him back again.

"Told you," I said."Just as well he's an infant, otherwise I could be so jealous."

Jason gave me a wonderful smile.

I dropped my voice. "Are we having dinner with my father tonight?"

"Not as yet. I plan to rectify that. But I *was* thinking we should meet him tonight. You know…maybe discuss him and Linda looking after Christopher."

I opened and closed my mouth. I didn't like the idea of my father and his potty wife looking after the baby.

"Let's go find Melody first," I said.

"You're right. Maybe she'll be sitting in Jean O'Hara's front parlour, drinking mint juleps, waiting for her next client to arrive."

"You think so?"

"No, I don't. Do you?"

I shook my head. We exchanged one more quick kiss then he took some cash out of the secret safe in his office and passed me some.

"Take it," he insisted.

He took some for himself and we left. I locked the office for him, pocketing the key. He'd never locked the office until he'd returned and found his private sanctum ransacked. There was evidence that somebody had tried tampering with his safe, but Jason had imported it from Europe before the war, and it required a complicated system of pass codes. The safe contained his private stash of money—not all of it, but I sometimes thought it was funny that the owner of a bank still hid his own money.

We walked up to the military check-in office on Nu'uanu Avenue, where residents could get gas masks and report lost items. It was papered with propaganda posters: *He Who Relaxes Helps The Axis. Get A Job!*

Remember Pearl Harbor?

How could we forget?

Two housewives stood out front, staring at a poster that read, *Women Can Help With The War!*

We walked in and waited as a family picked up their new gas masks.

"We need a gas mask," Jason said when we reached the counter.

The officer on desk duty put his hands on his hips.

"Did you lose yours again, Tinder?"

"No, sir." I held up the masks.

"It's for the baby," Jason responded.

"Oh, we don't have anything that small. Say, whose kid is this?"

"My sister's," I said. I was getting awfully comfortable with lying all of a sudden.

"Never knew you had one." He shook his head. "With babies this small, the mother is supposed to take turns breathing with him...or her." He jabbed a pen in the direction of the door. "I just took back two gas masks from a mother and child who are sailing home this afternoon. They've got a lot of children's things they're selling."

"Thanks," Jason and I said in unison. We knew exactly where to look. Kalakaua Avenue. Whole families had set up camp along the entire street on both sides selling off their household items.

We bought an English pram that had a blue canopy and big silver wheels from a woman who said she and her husband had snapped up the last two tickets for the weekly trip back to the mainland from the Matson offices in the Cook and Castle building over on Iwilei Road.

"Which ship are you going on?" Jason asked.

"I think they said it's the *Lurline*. We're very excited. Now my husband's on a warship, there's no need for us to be here." She looked away, embarrassed. "Do you think I'm a coward?"

"No," I said. *Yes.* It irked me that Honolulu had been fine and dandy for so many foreigners until disaster struck. I understood fear and panic. I'd done plenty of that myself in the first few days following the attack. But Honolulu needed her citizens. She needed her children's voices. She needed to know we still loved, cared for and believed in her.

"I need to see my family," the woman said.

And we needed a baby carriage. She also sold us a few other blankets and clothes she said the baby would grow into.

"Bon voyage," I said.

We put the baby in the British pram. He roared in fury when I pushed it. *Huh*. He gurgled like a guppy when Jason took over.

"What can I say?" my lover deadpanned. "I have the touch."

We walked to Jason's car, which was parked alongside a row of military-issue vehicles on Nu'uanu Street. We saw a sign tacked to a tree.

Businessmen of Hawaii Get Military Training Now! Kapiolani Park, January 25.

We'd seen these signs before. So far, the group had a few hundred men. They had asked Jason for a loan but baulked at the suggestion of him enroling in the planned Businessmen's Military Training Corps. So he had baulked at bankrolling their efforts. Already, many of their earliest members had dropped out—

either because they'd gone back to the mainland, joined the Army...or they didn't like the strict regulations. The term 'non Axis' had cropped up in just a few short weeks all over the country, not just the islands. In the islands, with such a close-knit group of people, it meant a lot of hurt feelings because anyone whose parents had come from what was deemed an 'enemy' nation was not welcome to join the BMTC. Jason was Chinese but still felt the group's collective cold shoulder. As a local white guy, I qualified, but they weren't interested in me, because I fraternised with Chinese people.

I saw the bleak expression on my lover's face.

"Jason...I love you," I said, desperate to see the smile back on his face. I got my wish. He blew me a quick kiss and shoved the fancy new pram in the back seat of his dusty, dinged-up black Delahaye 135 convertible. It had a couple of shell casings lodged in the trunk from the attack on Pearl Harbor. The pram would have been a lot easier to wedge inside it with the top down, but with the baby in the car we wanted to be careful. You never knew when the enemy might strike.

I held the baby in my arms, petrified when he started to wail. I'd prepared a bottle for him but it was difficult to feed him.

"You drive," Jason said, pulling over on Vineyard Avenue. We switched places. He took over feeding the baby and I took the wheel. He really had a knack for feeding Christopher. And I had a knack for finding good music. We grinned at each other when we heard the opening strains of *You Made Me Love You.*

* * * *

Jean O'Hara, Honolulu's most famous prostitute, had violated all the rules from day one when she landed at the harbour fresh off the boat from San Francisco. She'd been a working woman in Chicago, then California, and loved her work. She had a flair with men and happily shared her secrets with her closest gal pals, but red-haired Jean also had a temper. She got into spats with the police, military government officials, her own brothel madam and anyone else who got in her way.

I'd never actually met her, but of course I knew of her and I'd seen her driving around in her spanking new Zephyr at a time when prostitutes were forbidden to even *ride* in a vehicle, much less own one.

Both Jason and I sighed when we saw our beloved Waikiki Beach strewn with barbed wire. There were still some brave souls out there enjoying the sand and the sun. Not us, though. We were on a mission. I glanced at a Japanese restaurant sporting a huge sign: *We Brew SAKE only! No Rumours!*

I turned left, staggered at the amount of construction going on. Princess Kaiulani's exquisite estate had been chopped up for parts. I'd heard that there were plans afoot to turn it into hotels and residential homes.

We turned on Prince Edward Street and found Jean's blue house. It was a long, rectangular box. Its unassuming appearance surprised me. To my knowledge, up until now she'd been buying showy, expensive hilltop homes. Maybe she was trying to keep a low profile. To our surprise, we found a lot more construction going on here as well. Why were people building with the threat of attack hanging over our heads?

"Well," my lover reasoned, "with all the military personnel coming in and out of the islands, they need extra housing."

In the early days after the attack, all the wives and children of the officers from Schofield and Wheeler Field had been rounded up and held in temporary housing before being shipped back to the mainland. Very few had stayed but more and more high-ranking officers kept arriving. They needed somewhere to live and none of them would be caught dead cavorting with hookers in Chinatown.

"Her car's in the driveway," Jason said. "*Everybody* knows that's her car. She's just asking for trouble."

We walked up to the front door. Jean opened it. At least, it looked like Jean. She had red hair like Jean and wore a form-fitting red dress, but this woman was a mess. She stared at us from her one good eye. The other was swollen and half closed. When she opened her mouth, I could see some of her teeth were missing.

"Jean?" I blurted. Holy heck, she looked terrible. Now I knew why she didn't mind flaunting her car. She was in no shape to work. Her enemies had won.

For now.

"Who are you?" she asked.

"Tinder McCartney. And this is Jason Qui."

She gave me a sly smile. With her missing and broken teeth, it sort of gave me the creeps when she eyed me from stem to stern. "Oh...so *you're* Tinder. Wait...who the hell owns that kid?"

"Melody."

Her whole expression changed. "Not so loud," she hissed. "Get inside."

She ushered us into the dark interior. As ordinary as it looked outside, it was very nice inside, not that she seemed to have done much with it. She had a sofa and a couple of chairs. There was an open bottle of whisky on the coffee table, the only other piece of furniture. The house was in semi-darkness with its blackened windows. Everybody had blackened windows these days, but there was something very depressing about hers. I got the feeling she spent a lot of time in here on her own, nursing her injuries.

"Take the sofa," she said, flopping into a wing chair. I was right. I could see medicine powders, spoons and half-full glasses of water on the coffee table. I watched her hold an ice bag to her mouth.

"What happened to you?" I asked. I sat, but Jason was now on his knees on her hardwood floor, spreading a blanket and gently placing the baby on top of it before changing his diaper.

"We got a little visit from the police," she said. "We hadn't been open twenty-four hours when they stormed in here." She shook her head. "I had such a sweet house on Black Point. Shoulda stayed there."

"The police beat you up?"

"Not for the first time. We had a little disagreement over who controls me. One of them hauled off and slugged me. Three of them kicked me. They came in and stole some of my money and my booze. Wrecked my bridgework and knocked out my two front teeth. In case you're wondering, it hurts like fuck."

I was shocked at her coarse language. I'd never heard a woman talk like this but there was something about Jean that I liked.

"Why don't you go to the dentist?" I asked.

"Ha! Ha!" the baby chortled.

"I had a good one but he vanished after the attack and nobody else will work on a prostitute. Those cops left me for dead." She put back her head and closed her good eye.

"Don't worry, we have a good dentist. He'll work on you," Jason assured her.

She opened her eye again. "He'll work on a hooker?"

"He worked on me," I said. "Back when I was still tricking. He gave me nitrous oxide. I liked that a lot."

"I don't need that stuff," she said. "I have a high tolerance for pain." I had no doubt of that. "I think I might have a broken jaw. Can't eat a damned thing. Anything cold or hot in my mouth is fucking agony." She touched her cheek. "I've never felt anything like this. It goes all the way up my face and to my eye."

That explained her bizarre appearance.

"We'll take you to the dentist," Jason said. "But first, what happened to Melody?"

She hesitated. "She got scared when they beat up on her, too." She sat up, leaning on her elbows, her gaze on my face. "You may as well know—she married some military guy, he came here and sent for her, then changed his mind when she got off the ship. That girl fucked half the Army last time she was in town and nobody wasted any time telling him she was a harlot."

"How long has she been back on island?" I asked, using the local phrase.

"About a month. She came right over to me, said she needed work. We had a pretty good racket going on here, boys. She kept her kid in Chinatown and went over a few times a day to feed him. Sometimes she stayed over there because of curfew.

"I knew she wasn't handling things too good. She just wanted to be a wife and mom. Then came the raid." She picked up her whisky and took a slug. "I told that girl not to fall in love with the johns."

I gaped at her. "But she did?" I asked. "So soon?"

"Yeah. She did. She's gone and got herself a boyfriend. One of the mucky-muck military guys." Jean looked a little angry about this.

"Do you know who he is?"

"I can ask around. He was always comin' here and bringing her gifts. When we got raided, she called him and he came and took her away." She gestured to the baby and snorted. "I see she left behind a little something."

This story disturbed me. I didn't think Melody had abandoned her child. As we walked outside, my lover touched my elbow.

"I think she's in trouble, babe," he said in a low tone.

And I knew he wasn't talking about Jean. As she climbed into the car, I said, "Where's your gas mask?"

"Fuck my gas mask."

I couldn't help but laugh.

We drove her to King Street in Chinatown and she half lay in the back seat next to the pram, moaning as we drove.

Upstairs, the dentist greeted us. He asked me if I was staying out of trouble and laughed at his own joke. The last time I'd been here, I'd been assaulted in Chinatown and Jason had brought me here.

He took Jean into his office right away. He came out to us and said he thought she had a broken jaw. He ordered X-rays of the right side of her face and her mouth.

"Somebody took a good crack at her," he said.

Jean didn't want to go to the hospital. We could hear her screams from the waiting room. They suddenly stopped. We learned afterwards that he had given her some opium syrup to calm her nerves.

"I thought opium trading had been blocked," I told Jason as we got Jean down the stairs again. She was completely sedated…not that I minded. We had to go back up to retrieve the baby.

"Anything is possible in Chinatown," Jason said, when were back in the car, heading to Queen's Hospital. "It's the centre of all trading."

That was true.

Jean didn't snap out of her drug-induced stupor until we arrived at Queen's Hospital. Some of the uniformed men who knew her seemed to be horrified by her appearance.

"They're staring at me," she whimpered.

We got her inside the hospital and into the room with the big, giant X-ray machine. She was afraid of it.

The nurses were kind and kept a soothing demeanour as they prepared the machine for her. She lay on the bed, gazing up at us.

"We'll be right outside the door," I promised.

"You boys are so damned nice. You're queers, aren't you?" Before I could respond she slurred, "All the queers are damned fucking sweet."

The hospital staff knew her well. She'd been in plenty of times before. I took a peek at her hospital records and was shocked to see how many times she'd 'fallen down the stairs'. She'd been worked over by johns and cops alike over the last twelve months.

"If she were a boxer, they'd say she can take a good punch," one of the doctors told us. She got X-rays and found she had a broken cheekbone as well as a broken jaw.

"I'm going to give her sulphate antibiotics to help with the infection in her sinus. It's a short-acting antibiotic I have found very useful, particularly with her type of infection. We'll be doing surgery first thing in the morning."

"Don't tell anybody," Jean pleaded when we went to say goodbye. "I don't want anyone thinking I won't be back in business before long."

She would stay in the hospital overnight, receiving more pain management medication. With beds still needed for wounded soldiers, the staff was keen to have Jean out as soon as possible. Jason promised to pay cash for the surgery when we collected her the next day.

"I have money," Jean said. "I always pay my way. I'll pay you back."

She looked so pathetic as we waved goodbye and her bravado finally slipped.

"Don't leave me here," said the woman who had such a high tolerance for pain. "They'll finish me off for sure!"

We had to go. We had to find a home for Christopher before it got dark. We promised to return for her in the morning.

The duty nurse let me call my father from her desk phone. His tone was cautious when I reached him at his office.

"What's the matter? What's happened?"

"Nothing, Dad," I lied.

"You're in trouble."

"No." *Not really. I'm just stuck with a baby I can't look after.*

He reluctantly agreed to allow us to visit him. Jason and I drove back to Waikiki and to my father's store. As we walked down Liberty House's aisles, we both remarked how depressing it was to see nothing but functional clothing and useful building materials on display. It was eerie seeing mannequins with their gas masks on.

We saw a replica of Christopher's buggy along one wall. It was six times what we'd paid for it.

"Say, we know a bargain when we see one," Jason joked.

At my father's office, he was shocked when we strolled in with a baby.

"Whose is it?" he asked.

I was honest. I told him everything.

"Oh, boy. Linda will hate this," he said. "I know how she feels about hookers. On the other hand, she needs a project. This is perfect."

He jiggled the pram handle. The baby went nuts.

Jason took over again.

"You want some tea?" Dad asked. We wanted tea. "We just took delivery of some items from England. A warship came in yesterday with a lot of supplies. Most of it has been distributed to military families and the barracks, but I got to put my hands on a couple of things." He seemed very excited.

And just like that, I was starving again. It was now just after two o'clock and we had eaten nothing today but oranges for breakfast hours and hours ago.

Dad made us some English tea and I scarfed it down. We snacked on a couple of his imported arrowroot biscuits. Jason generously allowed me to dunk my biscuit in his tea since he was drinking like a gentleman.

We dawdled as long as we could. It was hard to say goodbye to Christopher.

My father was in a pretty good mood. I knew he'd bought a small house in Ainahaina from a departing family. He still had his house in Maui — or should I say, Linda's dream house — but he needed to be here.

"We'll have you over soon," he said. It sounded like a lie. We told him we wanted to have dinner the following evening. He said he would think about it.

Our little baby friend began to holler almost immediately when we got up to leave. Jason and I kissed his red, screwed up little cheeks and feverish, streaming eyes.

"It's just until we find Christopher's mother," I told Dad.

"Okay, I understand," he shouted over the screaming child. He kept jiggling the pram. I felt bad leaving him with just a few things.

"Oh, Linda will know what to get him," Dad shouted. We walked away, Jason and I both keeping our heads down.

"Why do I feel so damned lousy?" my man asked me outside the store.

"Because we hated leaving him."

"Yeah." He blew out a breath. "Come on, lover. Let me feed you, then I need to fuck you. We never did make it home for lunch."

"Yeah, I know." I fake pouted at him and we laughed. We drove over to Queen's Surf, one of the first restaurants he'd ever taken me to. It had picked up a lot of new clientele, mostly senior military, and had lost its slow, romantic service, which was to be expected. We ordered fish and chips and our meals arrived fast. We ate quickly, sipping on seltzer water. Underneath our small table, our legs touched. Our eyes connected. We were making our own romance. Suddenly, nothing else existed except this man and the waves crashing around on the cliffs below us.

A bird soared over our heads. Queen's Surf was like our favourite songs. It was a breather, a shade of calm.

It was a reminder that not everything in life came with barbed wire.

* * * *

We wandered back to the car. It seemed strange not to see Christopher's pram in the back seat. I took the wheel, Jason sitting beside me. He pressed my knee with a warm hand.

"You need to turn the key." His tone was gentle. I turned it, just like he suggested. I started to drive home, but I wanted to be out in the open with my man.

"Sweetheart, it's not safe," he said.

"Neither is being at home."

He couldn't argue with that. I took a detour to Princess Kaiulani's Ainahau estate. It was still open to the public but there wasn't much time before curfew so we had to hurry. I wanted him to experience my private oasis before the government tore it all up. Already, some of Kaiulani's heirs had sold off their plots of land. The bulk of the estate, including the beautiful house our last Princess had lived in, had been left as a public park to the Territory of Hawaii by Kaiulani's father after her untimely death. The Territory had declined the gift because maintaining it would be expensive. So, as they plotted and planned how to maximise its sale, parts of it kept getting chipped away.

"I've never spent much time here," my lover said. "Is this where you come and hide?"

"Yes." I smiled at him.

"Now I know where to look for you."

"I don't come here much anymore."

"But you know it's here." His tone was tender. His hand slid across my thigh, resting on my lap. "Oh, it's beautiful here. I wish I could buy this for you."

I laughed. I wished he could, too.

"My mother and I used to come here. This was her favourite place."

He squeezed my thigh. Hard. He knew how much I missed her.

He was filled with wonder at the lush estate, which had once been more than ten acres of wild paradise. Kaiulani's father, the former governor of Oahu, had planted every type of plant and flower imaginable here for the young Princess. A well-travelled man, he had found *pikake*, Chinese jasmine, in the Orient, and brought it all the way home by sea for his own delicate flower.

Today, people associated *pikake* with Hawaii and with Kaiulani, assuming the name was derived from her beloved peacocks that once roamed the grounds. Those birds, along with many of the estate's most exotic blooms, were all gone. I didn't like to think about what had happened to them. We parked near the house she had once called home and walked around my favourite area, the banyan tree that had been Kaiulani's sacred place. Most of it had been chopped down and replanted elsewhere, but some of it still survived.

I led him to the tree, which easily towered over us.

"It makes me feel so small," my lover said, peering up to its highest, bright green leaves. I pushed him between some of the strong aerial prop roots that shot down to the ground and came back up again, forming new life. Over and over again, we saw signs of determined life. The banyan tree had many rooted arms that looked odd, and yet seemed right. He ran his hands over the thick roots, mesmerised by their smooth strength and their will to survive. Even now, parts of the tree that had been severed were showing signs of regrowth.

"Now I know why you love it here," he said, kissing me. I pressed him against the host trunk. Our kisses grew more determined. I knelt before him, unbuckling his belt and lowering his pants as my lover pressed deep into the recesses of the tree. Unless anyone actually stood right over us, they never would have guessed I was sucking another man's cock.

His leaking, glistening head, beaded with his special brand of pearl nectar, bounced right against my lips. I pulled back and his cock twitched. I pursed my mouth into a kiss. It twitched again. With a small cry, Jason arched his hips forwards, anxious for contact. I allowed his cock past my lips instantly, working the slick head with long, flat licks until he grabbed my head and pushed his way deeper into my mouth. I reached between his hard thighs, stroking his taut ass cheeks, the crease between them and his sweet, heavy balls. I bobbed up and down, enjoying the little drops of juice I enticed from his cock. I reached a hand up and, underneath his shirt, began to caress his flat belly. He loved having me rub it when I sucked him, especially when he was standing.

"Oh, God, Tinder." He started rising up on his toes, another thing he did when he was standing up and getting the blow job from hell.

I took my mouth off him, ignoring his protests. I kept kissing his cock head and he kept shoving his sweet, moist shaft past my lips. I stayed on him as soon as I knew he was close. He grabbed a couple of tree roots and hung on for dear life when he erupted in my mouth.

He was on his toes, puffing and panting, then he almost fell on top of me.

"You just do it to me, Tinder. You…light fires in me. I don't know how to put them out."

"Yeah, but I do. That's my job." I stood, kissing him as I pulled his pants up and buckled his belt. I threw him over my shoulder and ran to our car.

"What are you doing?" he shouted, laughing.

"Getting you home before curfew. I want you naked. Right now."

Chapter Three

At our studio, we undressed one another with our usual intense rush. His hands moved all over my body, his expression serious as his fingers and tongue swept across my face and neck. I'd never been with such a sensual man. Jason got me hard just licking my face. He held my head in gentle hands, making a trail with his lips from my eyes, nose and mouth, moving to my philtrum, which he often told me was his favourite place on my body.

He licked the ridged space between my top lip and nose. He liked the name, philtrum, more than anything else — I think because it came from the Greek word, *philtron,* which means, according to him, 'love charm'.

Jason, in our most private moments, called me his love charm. His peppery kisses traversed my collarbone and back up to my shoulders. My cock was rock hard now and I would have let it go further except curfew was coming. Better to be safe than sorry. We worked our way around the large room and made sure the black curtains were all in place. The kitchen and bathroom were no exception. We lit two small candles by the bed and, before I could kiss my man's beautiful face, he dropped to his knees in front of me. He kissed my cock head. It reacted to his mouth, twitching against his tongue.

I groaned. I loved the way he sucked me. He kept his mouth tight, pulling back. He released me with a popping sound.

"God, I love you, Tinder," he said and swallowed my cock again. Sucking, pulling, teasing, tasting... He released me and kept putting kisses up and down my shaft, driving me mad with the promise of things to come.

He pushed me back on to the bed. Jason sighed against my thigh and opened up my legs by tossing them up and pinning them to my chest. I could feel his shoulder moving against the back of my thigh and knew he was stroking his own cock. *Oh, God, yes.* He was going to fuck me.

Jason sucked my ass. He sometimes sucked it for hours. I came inside his mouth many times, but coming with his cock inside me beat everything. He had discovered lubrication gel in a Chinese chemist and we used it from time to time, but for us nothing beat hand to mouth to cock contact.

He couldn't wait and neither could I. He got between my legs, his cock rigid.

"I dream of fucking you," he said. "Sometimes, it's all I think about."

"Me, too. I hate when you leave the house without me now."

He blinked. "I know you do, baby." His cock started poking at my hole. I was still slick and wet from his tongue, but as always, half the fun was Jason working his way into me. It saddened me that women can get wet for their men but we men cannot.

Jason leant down on me, balancing himself on his palms and knees, his hips swivelling the way they always did when he was anxious to fuck me. I yearned for the feeling of fullness I always got when he was inside me. The tremor of pain that began when his cock moved into me eased right away and he began thrusting faster, harder—desperate for complete submersion. We'd been fucking when Pearl Harbor was attacked. Now we fucked like each minute might be our last. He kissed my mouth, his tongue dipping against mine. He moved down to suck my nipples, my knees pinned hard between his chest and mine.

He fucked me with relentless strokes. I held on to his rutting ass. I loved the way he fucked me, like I was the last man left on earth.

"Come with me," he said, his voice a hypnotic command. I had to do his bidding. I felt the orgasm surge deep within me, little sparks of light turning to bright fires. He came deep inside my ass, my left nipple in his mouth. I came between us, the juices coating my chest and belly. He eased off his aggressive pace and licked the trail I'd left behind.

"See how hard you come when I make you wait?" he asked.

Denied twice today, I saw spots before my eyes. I could only nod, unable to speak. He kissed my mouth.

"Catch your breath, baby," he murmured. "Papa's not finished with you yet."

* * * *

We'd fucked all night, until the whine of patrol planes overhead acted as a reminder that we had a long day ahead of us. He rolled off me, holding me in his arms. We'd started to drift off, too exhausted to even worry when there was a fire drill. We heard it, but our arms just tightened around one another. As I'd fallen asleep, my face in Jason's hair, my last thought was that he smelt just like Christopher.

I had no idea how long we'd been asleep, but Jason's nightmares returned.

"No, no,! *Jiù méi ting*! Stop!"

He thrashed about, his arm hitting me in the head. I sat up, fumbling for the bedside lamp on his side of the bed. His face was a mask of terror.

I tried to calm him. My lover's dark, haunted eyes stared up at me, tears leaking from them.

"Did I hurt you?" This was always his first question and, as usual, I said no. I wanted him to release the terrors in his brain without worrying about me.

"I can't remember his name," Jason whispered. "How can I pray for him when I don't remember?"

His tears tore at me and I fought off my own. This was more than he'd ever said about what had happened to him after he had been captured. The night terrors had started as soon as he came home. He always shouted the same thing.

"You can pray for him," I said, wishing I could ask questions to draw more from him, but questions would make him wake up and once he was fully conscious he would shut down.

Scooting beside him, I spooned him, rubbing his body with a gentle touch. "You can pray and tell him you think of him. What…does he look like?"

"Young…blond… Tinder, he looked so much like you. If you…if anything happens to you…"

His muffled sobs broke my heart. I kissed his hair that smelt like Fairy soap and rocked him to sleep with my body. It always worked. His body trembled and shook, then finally let go of the awful dream. Jason slept and I remained awake, so worried about him. In daylight he never talked about the dreams. It was as if they never happened.

He got up to leave me at five as usual. It worried me because it was officially curfew until daybreak. I wanted to go with him, as had been my new determination, but he kissed my still-closed eyes.

"Sleep, baby. I'll be right back."

* * * *

Thursday, January 22, 1942

Somebody began knocking at our door at six a.m. and kept knocking until I got up from our bed, threw on my trousers from the day before and opened the door. I panicked that something had happened to Jason. He was usually back by now. My heart pounded in my chest as I stood there, surprised to see my father, who began to wheel the pram with a squealing Christopher inside.

Jason came running down the alley towards us, looking nervous.

"What's going on?" From where he stood, he looked over my father's shoulder, staring down at the infant.

Jason helped Dad bring in the baby after handing me a bag full of groceries and a wrapped package from the laundry. The moment we closed the door, my dad began to babble.

"I got you some formula and more diapers. Linda can't cope and I don't have time for a baby." My father put the bag onto a chair. "What time's dinner? You're getting me the best steak money can buy."

Jason plucked the baby out of the pram and rocked him in his arms. It was the same way I rocked Jason to sleep when he experienced night terrors.

"Around five?" I asked, since my lover had become gaga over the kid. Dad was still rambling. It was so unlike him. I knew he had to be very upset. Jason turned, gave me a quick kiss even though he knew my father hated to see signs of affection between us, then took the groceries in his free hand and wandered off to the kitchen.

"I'll make coffee," he said over his shoulder. "I'll show Christopher how."

That made me laugh.

"He's pretty good with him," Dad said, shutting the door. He peered at all the chairs and the antique red velvet sofa we had acquired. He was spoilt for chairs, since we had so many, but sat instead on the edge of our bed.

"How is she doing?" I sat beside him, discreetly checking my fly, making sure I wasn't showing my father any naked bits.

"She's...okay. I've realised something about that woman."

"Yeah, what's that?"

"She has a desperate need to be the centre of attention at all times."

I grinned. "You *just* noticed that?"

He shot me a bleak look. "I know you don't like her."

"Oh, Dad." I shook my head. He'd been so blind to her machinations, but then, she had always been okay with him. She was mean to me, and especially to Jason. I knew she was narcissistic and selfish. I'd recognised those qualities immediately in his new wife. She'd been his hot little mistress as my mother lay dying of cancer. Linda had been his refuge.

Of course, she'd played her cards right until my mom had passed and then she'd put the bite on him to marry her. My father, I had realised some time ago, must have loved my mother a lot. He loved being married, loved being a husband. He got married again because he was in love with the state of wedded bliss, not because he was in love with Linda.

For me, it had been a shock discovering she even existed. Then to add insult to injury, he had introduced me to her and at the same time told me they were getting married and moving to Maui. He'd sold my childhood home and all our furnishings. I had still been dealing with the loss of my mother, who'd died as I was crossing the Pacific from San Francisco to be with her. I guess, in his own way, my father had been dealing with her loss, too, by trying to replace her. I could have told him you can never replace people.

"What am I going to do, Tinder?"

I didn't know how to respond. He knew I didn't like her and the Lord knew I'd tried to get along with her. I'd even saved her from a suicide attempt. I looked at him. "What's going on, Dad?"

He shook his head. "She's crazy. She wanted to get an exorcist to drive the devil out of the baby."

Jason stood in the doorway, a plate of Chinese pastries in his hand. The shock of what he'd heard registered on his face.

I stood, moving over to him. I took the plate from his fingers before it fell. The baby was asleep, his head on Jason's shoulder. I stroked the sweet little boy's back, then took the plate over to our tightly wedged dining table.

"Come and take a seat, Dad." I pointed out the delicacies my lover had brought home. "This rice dumpling is Nuo Mi Zi." I checked the see-through ball and it was red in the centre. "It has lotus seed paste in the middle. Right, Jason?"

Jason nodded and turned on his heel.

"And these round ones are called cocktail buns. They have coconut in them. And these," I looked up and smiled at Dad, "are my favourites." I pointed to the round, two-inch cake with pastry edging and Chinese writing on top. "They're called mooncakes."

Jason joined us, somehow managing a tray with the coffee pot and cups while still holding the baby.

"They traditionally sell mooncakes in the fall, but they've been making them early at the bakeries here because, in the Chinese tradition, eating mooncake stops bad things from happening. They're supposed to bring great good luck."

"Really?" My father picked one up. "It feels heavy." He bit into it, his face morphing into different expressions. "Oh, wow…it's sweet and savoury and…" He took his mouth away from it. "Is that an egg inside it?"

Jason nodded. He turned Christopher around and fed him a bottle as I poured out coffee.

"I can see why you like these," my father said. "I like the custard inside it."

Dad and I were custard guys. We grinned at each other.

"How is his poop this morning, Dad? Still green?"

My father stopped eating. "Thanks, Tinder. I need to think about poop when I'm eating."

I shrugged. "Everybody poops, Dad."

"Not listening." He closed his eyes and bit into his mooncake.

Jason sipped his coffee and I could feel his thigh moving slightly under the table to touch mine. We exchanged hot looks. By now, were we alone, we'd be rolling around our sheets having hot monkey sex. I tried not to think of his nightmares, of his hidden anguish.

"You've become so…Eastern ever since you met Jason," my father said. I didn't disagree with him, but the truth was I'd embraced Chinese culture before I met my man. I'd already been living in Chinatown. I took a deep breath. I was so glad I wasn't getting ready to service a bunch of sailors today. The female prostitutes handled a minimum of a hundred men a day. I had no idea how they did it.

When I didn't say anything, my father said, "What are you going to do about the kid?"

"We're going to look for Melody," Jason said, his gaze sliding over to me. I nodded in confirmation. "We don't want to go to the police since this involves the military." He paused. "It also involves some kind people in Chinatown who tried to help a working girl. Everybody Asian is terrified of getting into trouble. There's so much talk of Axis and non-Axis families…the threat of internment camps… No, we'll begin our inquiries in a discreet way."

My father put his elbows on the table and leaned towards us. "I think you're quite right. I really don't like the undertones of exclusion. When you and Tinder were declined for the Businessmen's Military Training Corps… I will be frank—I assumed, incorrectly, that they knew you are homosexual and disapproved."

"Dad," I said, "We are beyond discreet. We're—"

He held up a hand. "Tinder, I know. I applied also. I, too, was rejected."

Jason made a low moan in his throat. I just about exploded.

"What?"

Dad shrugged. "Tinder, you and I were rejected because we are white. We're locals, but that's the new discrimination. We're Hawaiian but now they are calling us *haole*."

"But *haole* are foreigners."

He sounded exasperated when he said, "We're still not Hawaiian in their eyes. I know it doesn't make sense, son. I didn't say it did."

We each sat, silent for a moment.

My father said, his voice very low, "Put on the radio. I have something to tell you."

Now he was worried about being overheard when he'd just been waving around the word homosexual?

I turned on the radio and Christopher gave a shout of approval to Artie Shaw.

"There is a new group of volunteers that will also be trained by Army soldiers," my father said as soon as I sat down again. "This group is called the Hawaii Defence Volunteers and all nationalities are welcome. There are Japanese-Americans, Chinese, Filipinos, Puerto Ricans, Koreans and, of course, white people."

We didn't say anything for a moment.

"You want us to join?" Jason asked.

"Yes." My father picked up his cup. "I think the more of us who are trained for combat, the better."

"I agree," Jason said.

"Good thing, because there's a meeting at my house tomorrow morning."

This was the first invitation we'd had to my father's house and I would have said yes to anything just to go there. I loved my father in spite of his crazy wife and his inherent disapproval of my relationship.

He hugged me for what seemed like several minutes before he left. Jason put the baby in the pram whilst we bathed. We longed to fuck each other but Dad had delayed our start for the day.

As we left our studio with everything we'd need for the day, one of our neighbours came out of his apartment and stopped us.

"I want to join the volunteers," he whispered. He put his finger to his lips and ran back inside again. So much for the music covering up our conversation.

Jason and I first went to the bank so he could sign some papers, then checked on the laundries and dry cleaners before we took the Pali Road over the hill into the windward side of the island. Here, the war was not so much a constant reminder. The vibe was much more relaxed, even though we passed several truckloads of uniformed men heading for Schofield Barracks.

Those barracks were a sore point with me. Some of the buildings had been bombed out and were being rebuilt. I'd offered to help but was declined.

Jason had assured me there was plenty I could do and I had learned that he was right. We veered off the Pali Road to the Old Pali Road. Jason was holding the baby, who slept even when we parked beside the abandoned Palmer Orchards. The others were here already. Jason took out the pram and propped the baby inside it as I reached into the trunk for our work gloves.

We greeted the six volunteers who met here twice a week and we began picking peaches, lemons and oranges from the tree. Everybody had the same question.

"Whose kid is it?"

We stuck to our story about a sister. Nobody questioned it. Christopher lay in his pram, staring up into the shady canopy of leaves as we worked.

Occasionally, I'd see a few of the guys go over and check on the baby if he made a noise or just for a bit of respite. He was having a wonderful time and had kicked off his covers. I went over to check on him and his little feet landed on my lips. He giggled. I laughed back at him. I caught my lover's smile. Having the little guy here as we worked was a reminder of hope. It cheered us all up, even though little was said.

Twenty-two boxes were filled. Our group leader, Sam Kaonaka—a big, wonderful Hawaiian guy— needed one more. Jason and I scrambled to fill it with a mixture of fruit.

"Okay, you three," he said, indicating, me, Jason, and Christopher, "You take four boxes over to Schofield Barracks. Did you get some fruit for your family?"

Christopher started to fuss.

"I'll get the fruit," Jason said. "You take care of the baby."

Sam distributed the remaining boxes to be taken to other bases around the island. And I began to panic about taking care of the baby.

Oh, joy. Only Jason could calm the little guy. I walked over to him, surprised when he smiled at me. He knew me! I realised he was a smart kid. Jason had seemed familiar to him because he was Chinese and a Chinese family had looked after him. I picked him up and cuddled him. Jason picked enough fruit for us to share with my father and our neighbours. He packed up our car then he took the wheel as I held the baby.

We headed back across the Old Pali Road and down towards Honolulu.

When the gate guards saw our car, their faces split into grins.

"Hey," one of them said, sticking his face into the passenger window, "I can smell the peaches from here." He ruffled the baby's head. "Cute kid."

The guards waved us past the first checkpoint and we stopped at the second. It was only our fourth time doing this but the guards knew us.

"You should get a basket for the little guy," one of them said, helping Jason who hefted out a box of fruit. "You can put him in a basket on the floorboards."

I stared at him. I was not putting our child on the floorboards...in a basket, no less.

Wait...he is not our child. I felt forlorn suddenly and held the baby just a little bit tighter.

Back in the car, Jason waited until we'd left the property to say, "Sweet Tinder, you should see the expression on your face."

I looked at him. "Do we have to give him up?"

Jason pulled over as quickly as he could. He leaned over and kissed me.

"God, I hope not. Tinder, I love seeing you with him. You've never looked sexier to me."

"Can we...you know...two men...can we raise him?"

"Why not?" He shrugged and moved back on to the road again. "We may want to think about some help."

I was quiet for a moment. A nanny. That would be good. But we had so little room.

Our next stop was the hospital.

"Are you coming to take her home?" the desk duty nurse asked. "Because that woman is impossible."

Jean O'Hara had come out of surgery and was very grumpy.

"See here," she said. "You *have* to take me to the dentist. I need my teeth fixed and since I'm still out of it, now is the perfect time."

"Take her, take her," the nurse urged, handing me packets of pain pills for Honolulu's most notorious hooker. We took her down to King Street.

I sat in the car waiting for Jason, who helped her up the stairs for her dental surgery. He came back down, a look of shining happiness on his face.

"Tinder, she wants to sell her house. I told her we'd buy it. She paid cash for it. I told her we'd pay her a little more. We're supposed to pick her up at three o'clock, so I'll have the contract drawn up right now."

"What will she do? Buy another house?"

"She wants to go to Maui. I told her we'd help get her off island. She doesn't want to be seen all beat-up like this."

"How are we going to do that?"

Jason looked around, saw nobody in sight, then kissed me.

"The fisherman who helped you find me. I bet we can talk him into it. She *really* wants to get off this island."

We discussed the house and Jean's move all the way to the bank, where he prepared the documents and put together the cash. He found a chair for me in one of the other offices. Christopher and I sat across from him, watching him work.

"Jean bought a brand new house for fair market value," he said, consulting a land map he used in studying loan applications. Honolulu was changing every week with the sudden boon in building. "We'll have a house that has lots of rooms. Plenty of room for a nanny." He looked at me. "And for your father."

That startled me. "My *father*?"

Jason nodded. "I suspect his problems with his wife are worse than we thought."

"But—"

"Tinder." His voice was gentle. "I'm just saying. He has a place to come home to if need be."

I said nothing for a moment. I was constantly amazed by Jason's generosity.

"This is a new house. It has so many possibilities for us." He smiled. "I just got in a new application for funding on a three-unit lot right next door to us. It hasn't been approved by the war office yet or assigned to a construction company. The loan has come from the owner of the land, but I think he'd be happy to sell it to us for a good price.

"We could bankroll the construction…take over the project."

"We?"

"You and I are a team, baby. I can't do this without you. You can be the architect and we can build it. We'll make it a family business. Nobody can say no to us anymore." He smiled. "We can also choose our own neighbours."

I stared at him. "Can you do that?"

"Watch me."

And just like that, Jason and I got ourselves a brand new house, and a new business venture.

* * * *

We went to see my father at Liberty House and gave him some of our fruit. He looked pleased. "I'll give some of these to the staff and Linda can have a couple of peaches. She loves these peaches," he said, a faint look of desperation in his eyes. "Thank you, boys."

We still had errands to run but told him we would meet him at five. We found our fisherman down at the Market Street wharf. He was happy to help a pretty woman—Jason's words, not mine—get to Maui the following morning. *Pretty woman?* Wait until he got a load of her mashed and swollen face and she snapped at him a time or two.

"Real pretty, huh?"

"Yes," Jason lied, paying him in cash.

Jean was half out of her mind on opium when we collected her. "When am I going to Maui?" she bleated.

"Tomorrow morning."

She sat in the back seat, moaning a little more. Her jaw had been wired, her face packed with gauze. She looked worse than she had the day before.

"You got my cash?"

"All of it," Jason answered.

"Why can't I go today?"

"Curfew soon and, besides, he's a fisherman. He always sets out first thing in the morning. Don't worry, we'll bring you to him," Jason said.

"What's his name?"

"Tsi San Lo."

"I'm gonna stink of fish."

"That's the least of your worries," Jason said.

She actually laughed. She didn't seem happy about the delay but just sighed a couple of times, putting her hand to her face.

"Are you in a lot of pain?" I asked. "I have your pills from the hospital." She took them from me.

"I have something much better from the dentist." She opened a small brown bottle that contained some drops, squirted it into her mouth and leant back.

"I can see why field workers love opium syrup," she said, her speech very slurred. "I—" With her sentence unfinished, she dropped right to sleep.

My lover touched my thigh and blew me a kiss. I blew one back.

* * * *

At her house, she combed through the papers, signed them with a flourish, and grinned at us.

"Hope you have more fun here than I did," she said. "Not that I've done more than screw, sleep, and drink. Which reminds me..." She took out the brown bottle and twisted the cap open.

"What is the name of Melody's new boyfriend?" Jason asked quickly, holding the cash she wanted in his hands. She looked from the money to him and back again.

"Walter Stevenson. He's married. Like I said yesterday, he's a big mucky-muck."

I'd never heard of the guy and neither had Jason.

"He came every day once he arrived on island. Been here a few weeks. Came without his family."

"But you knew he was married?" Jason asked.

"Sure I did. He wore his wedding ring." She must have seen Jason's look of surprise. "Don't think the johns care about our feelings. We're not mistresses, or girlfriends. We're whores. They don't care if we know they're married."

"Are they good in the sack?" I asked.

"Not most of them." She grinned at me then grimaced. "Melody left some things in her room," she suddenly said. "Not very much, really, but you might want to check and see if she left anything useful. Last room on the right, just down the hall."

Jason and I looked at each other. He handed her the cash, and she placed it on her lap then squeezed some syrup into her mouth. Her eyes started to droop. She swung her legs onto the sofa, lay down and closed her eyes.

"I have to be back here in six weeks," she murmured. "My new bridge comes in. Then I'll look beautiful again. I'm gonna get me a mucky-muck."

We started to walk through the house.

The only rooms that appeared to have been in use were the living room, kitchen, bathroom and Jean's bedroom, which was a mess.

Down the hall were the dining room that was empty, a second bedroom, empty linen closets, a second bathroom and, at the very end, what must have been Melody's bedroom.

We found lots of white wax melted in dishes on a small nightstand next to her bed. There was a wardrobe with a few dresses and a suitcase. Inside this, we found her shipping ticket. She'd sailed on the SS *Matsonia* – a Matson company ship that had previously been called the *Malolo* before dry-docking for refitting a few years ago. It had been used in the last year to transport troops and their families to and from the islands.

Her passage had been ticketed under the name of Melody Hampton.

"Was that her married name or maiden name?" Jason asked me. I had no idea.

We found little else of use.

"Wonder what she did with the wax," Jason commented. "She burned down a lot of it."

"Her teeth," Jean said from the doorway.

We both turned.

"She had a lot of cavities. She hid them by filling them in with wax."

Jason and I looked at each other then thanked her for letting us see the room and told her we'd pick her up in the morning.

She snorted. "Not me. I'm heading over there now. I've gotta find me some better transportation."

"Aren't you in pain?"

"Yes. Here's your key, boys." She tossed us the key. "You can have the furniture. We'll call it a house-warming present. I gotta hide my car. Goddam cops bashed out my fog lights," she shouted over her shoulder as she walked out of the door. A few minutes later, we watched Jean backing her car down the driveway. We waved from the doorstep then walked back inside. She'd taken all her personal belongings, not that there had been much. I could still feel her presence, though. Jean was quite a character.

"Think she's got a little place somewhere else?" I asked Jason.

"I wouldn't be surprised."

The baby, who'd been asleep in his pram in the living room, began to squawk. Jason fed him while I checked the house for things we'd need. Half the rooms had no light bulbs. The bathroom was a mess. I laughed when I looked at the cabinet mirror and saw that Jean had left us a great big sticky kiss in her trademark red lipstick.

My lover came to the door. "Babe, you're never going to believe it but the people across the road are moving out. They're selling off a baby crib!"

I believed it. Somehow, we were on a voyage of our own. Jason and I were in our own little boat. I wondered if fish would be involved. As I thought about the military tribunal coming up next week, I got the chilling image of the two of us being circled by sharks.

Chapter Four

We met my father at Liberty House. He and Linda were waiting out front, all dressed up, and seemed excited we were taking them out. She was in such a good mood she patted my shoulder as we took off.

"Thank you for the peaches. I'm going to make a pie!"

"Glad you like them," I said. None of us mentioned the baby who lay in my arms, miraculously asleep as Jason drove. She and Dad acted as if he wasn't there.

"Where are we going?" Dad asked.

"A new restaurant that just opened up in Wahiawa," Jason said.

I already knew he wanted to check on his new investment, Michel's — a French restaurant owned and operated by a cute little Frenchman of the same name. He had approached Jason the first week we'd returned to Honolulu. Being a foreigner, the man was worried about getting financing from an American-owned bank on the island. Jason was only too happy to help.

"Wahiawa?" Linda sounded doubtful. Located in the central valley of Oahu, this sleepy, quiet, peaceful town had the funny name of Wahiawa—Hawaiian for 'Place of Noise'. It had once been so quiet people said they could hear the sounds of the ocean from both sides of the coast. Now it was surrounded by military bases.

Jason thought Michel was smart to provide French food in such an unusual place. In spite of heavy military presence, there was a serenity to the area. We drove over the only road leading to the town, oohing and aahing as we passed one of the few lakes on the island, Kaukonahua.

When we arrived at the airy restaurant on Wilikina Drive, we were charmed by the place—and by the smell.

"Onion soup," Linda said, sniffing appreciatively.

Michel came out to greet us. He seemed to like Jason and shook his hand repeatedly. Being French, he reserved his extra special charm for Linda and she gobbled up the attention. After greeting us, he gave us hand-printed menus and once we'd ordered he raced off to the kitchen.

"He does all the cooking and table waiting himself," Jason said. "He told me he works fourteen-hour days and it is nothing to him."

Linda played with her cutlery. "He has more stamina than your father, Tinder. He comes home and falls asleep the moment he walks through the door."

I saw my father's face fall. He was probably exhausted when he came home from work.

"Any news on shipments?" Jason asked, wisely changing the subject.

"As you know, we've got more and more servicemen coming into Honolulu every week. Sailors, soldiers…supplies of everything are limited. I've been talking to the Matson cargo office in San Francisco, and they've just been authorised to send over a shipment next week. We should have it five days after that."

That had been the company's motto for its exotic cruises, but with everyday supplies being so low on the islands, this shipment would be essential. My father looked worried. Three Matson cargo ships had already been bombed, including Jason's.

"Things have to get better," Jason said. "I really think they will."

Michel bustled out with glasses of water. He seemed so pleased that Jason had come to dinner and had even prepared the baby's bottle of formula in the kitchen for him.

"What do you plan to do with that child?" Linda finally acknowledged Christopher.

"Look after him. We don't know where his mother is. We—"

"He's a prostitute's baby," she hissed.

"His mother is married to a military man."

"She's married?" Linda shot a withering look at Dad. "He didn't mention that."

"She *was* a working girl," I explained. Michel came out with our food, then, after he had fussed over our most immediate needs, left us alone.

"It's not Christopher's fault he has a mom who was a working girl. No baby should be abandoned because of his parents'…mistakes."

She said nothing, tucking into her food. She seemed in a better mood as she sipped her soup. "It's really very good."

It annoyed me that she sounded so surprised.

We motored through the huge and hearty bowls of soup and gigantic portions of steak and potatoes. I ate everything, even my vegetables. I eyed Linda's peas in a predatory way as she pushed them around the plate.

"I hate Hawaii," she suddenly said.

Nobody had a response. I glanced at my father who was staring up at the ceiling, as if looking for guidance. The cheque came and when Michel brought her a little plate of cookies, Linda seemed to cheer up.

Jason paid for our meals and we shuffled outside.

"Drive slow past the lake," Linda said. "This whole island was once like this." She started to cry.

I was heartily sick of her. None of us *liked* what was happening, but she had it better than most.

We dropped my father and Linda at their house in Ainahaina. It was a short drive back to the house on Prince Edward Avenue. Although we still didn't have most of our things, we had enough to get by for one evening. We didn't want to run the risk of breaking curfew.

Jean might have pooh-poohed having a gas mask but she had done a good job of blacking out the windows. The only thing we really hated about curfew was being quiet. We sometimes listened to our radio music on a very low volume in our studio but we weren't sure about our neighbours here, yet.

We hadn't given much thought to selecting a bedroom for ourselves but ended up choosing Jean's, as it was the biggest. She'd left her bed, which was surprisingly comfortable, and she'd left a set of sheets in the linen closet. They would do for tonight.

As I bathed and clothed the baby, Jason made lists of things we needed to do.

I spent the evening cleaning as he rocked the baby in his new crib in our room. Our little guy fell asleep at last and Jason tiptoed out to the kitchen where I was cleaning out the fridge.

"Guess she found a pretty good use for her gas mask," Jason joked. I looked inside it. It was filled with cigarette stubs. She'd been using it as an ashtray.

We had a good laugh about that, then worried about making noise. We shushed each other with kisses.

"I want you," Jason said.

"I want you, too."

We were afraid to make noise in our room and awaken the baby and, frankly, we were afraid of him watching us. We kept discussing it in hushed tones.

"He's three months old," I said. "He won't remember."

"Are you sure?"

In the end, the sofa proved to be a very comfortable place. We stripped off before attacking one another with our mouths. I pushed my lover to the sofa and squatted between his open thighs. I took my time sucking his cock. I lingered over the head with my tongue and lips. He moaned as I sucked him back into my mouth, taking him all the way to the base. My nose nuzzled his sweet-smelling pubic hair. Lord, I loved everything about the man.

I lifted my face when he grabbed my chin.

"Look what I found stuffed down the pillows, baby!"

It was a tube of K-Y Jelly.

"Turn around, Tinder."

I turned. His tongue began to stroke its way along my butt cheeks and up into the crevice. I held my breath, waiting for the moment his tongue hit my hot spot. He made me wait. I found myself bending forwards, holding the coffee table for support. I tried to get his face where I needed it. He was so sneaky. His tongue would find me, flicker at my hole then move away.

He became as excited as I was. Suddenly his tongue was on me, in me, stoking fires in me as only he could do. He snapped the cap on the jelly then his fingers smeared the cold stuff on me. I jumped a little. He was so worked up that his hard cock poked at me. He grabbed my hips and worked it into me. I was on my knees, begging for it. Jason started slamming into me, taking me from behind. This was one of my favourite ways for him to fuck me. His cock hit me in all the right places in this position and he knew it. I loved the way he dominated me in this position and the way his balls slapped against my ass.

Fuck…

I was about to come and wanted to grab my cock, but Jason beat me to it. He jerked on me with expert fingers. I felt his cock getting bigger inside my belly the way it always did when he fucked me this way and we came hard, together. Just as we finished, Jason's kisses raining on my shoulders, the baby started to cry.

Jason laughed as he pulled out of me. "He's got good timing. At least he waited."

* * * *

Friday, January 23, 1942

We awoke later than usual. Jason panicked at first because he was late opening his stores.

"I guess I'm going to have to let them have the keys," he said, but he didn't look happy about it. The workers were able to lock up without keys, but not enter the stores.

"Let's go," I said. We began to get ready. I was surprised and delighted that he hadn't had a nightmare during the night—not that I said anything. We had no food for us and only a tiny bit of formula left for the baby, so we bathed and re-dressed in the same clothes from yesterday and headed back to Chinatown.

Having not been in this part of the city early in the morning, we hadn't realised just how many servicemen there were in Honolulu and how listless most of them seemed. A bunch of enlisted men were clustered on Kau Kau Korner, reading the morning papers. They all waved at us. We waved back. Wow, they looked so bored.

The truth was, there was little to do in Honolulu and, outside of Chinatown, almost nothing, in fact. Chinatown itself did its best to entertain the troops but its resources were strained. My eyes bugged when we parked and walked down Nu'uanu. There were men everywhere. A few had got hold of bicycles and clowned around on them. Drivers were having to inch around them but nobody honked or jeered.

To all of us in the islands, the uniformed men were friendly invaders.

"More guys than ever," Jason remarked. They lolled about everywhere, in doorways and in shops, doing nothing. We opened the businesses and kept moving. A few sailors stopped us.

Most seemed sober, which was a blessing, but some looked like they'd already downed a few drinks.

"What can we do?" they asked. "There's nothing to do."

At night, some of the men slept on their ships since the accommodations in Honolulu were non-existent and some of the destroyed barracks were still under repair. The men came ashore by day. They had energy to burn.

"I heard all about the nekkid hula dancers and the hot honeys," one said.

"Yeah, and the hot whores," another guy said.

"All you do is line up for everything, even the whores…and when I finally got up those damned stairs, she was a rough bit of road. It was like having sex with my grandma."

We laughed. We couldn't help it. What they said was true, but what could we do about it?

We suggested Wo Fat's, the popular Chinese restaurant. Kau Kau Korner was also popular for cheeseburgers and shakes. We suggested ice skating at the Waikiki Skating Arena on the corner of Kalakaua and McCully.

"You like to swim?" Jason asked. "There's always the beach. The Natatorium used to be a great place to swim, but the Army's taken it over for training exercises."

"Naw," one of them said. "I kinda got my heart set on a nekkid hula girl."

"Do they exist?" somebody else asked.

Jason and I looked at each other, shook our heads and the guys collectively sighed. They thanked us and kept on…doing nothing.

We pushed past dozens of them while walking down to the studio. I was stunned to see a sleek black car waiting outside for us. At least I assumed it was for us. It completely blocked our entry.

A man in uniform sat in back. He rolled down his window.

"Is that her kid?"

"Whose?" Jason asked.

"You know who."

"Where is she?" Jason countered.

The man sneered. "Answer the question."

"You answer first."

The man shrugged. "On her way back to the mainland. She's been arrested."

"For what?" I asked.

"She doesn't want the kid and neither do I," he said. "Keep this to yourself."

He rolled up the window and the car almost drove over our feet as the driver took off.

"She's been arrested?" I asked Jason.

He shrugged. "We'll soon find out."

We looked at each other. It was time to make a trip to the police. We stopped on the way to hand in Jean O'Hara's gas mask, which I'd cleaned up, at the military check-in office.

"Have you lost your mask again, Tinder?" the desk sergeant asked the second he saw me. I held up my mask so he could see it before handing over Jean's.

Jason waited outside for me, the baby with him. I had walked out to join them when a family rushed in, returning their gas masks. Off to the side stood a young woman in a traditional Japanese kimono. She looked beautiful but it was an unusual sight to see a young woman in such attire. Even her hair was lacquered and bore traditional kanzashi kogai sticks and an ornamental fan. She stood, holding a small suitcase, looking terribly distressed. She seemed to be fighting off tears.

I stared at her.

"Are you all right?" I asked her. She looked petrified and let out a little peep of fear when the family rushed back out again.

"Come on, Sasumi," the woman said, tugging the girl's hand. "You have to come inside. You have to register with the government."

"What's going on?" I asked when the girl began to quietly sob.

"We're going back to the mainland and she can't come with us. She's Japanese. They've already started rounding people up on the mainland and putting them in internment camps."

"But they're not doing that here," I said, startled by her matter-of-fact manner.

"No, but we can't take her with us and she probably won't get work. She'll have to go stay with a government host family until they figure out what to do with her."

That sounded gruesome.

"I…am…American," the girl said, her voice sounding strong in spite of her tears.

"Yes, I know you are," the woman said, dragging her inside.

The children of the family began to sob.

"Jason," I said, "We need a nanny."

He looked at me. "I don't know if we can, Tinder."

"Please, please," the children began to chant. They ran inside the office, pointing at us. The desk sergeant urged us in.

"You can give her a job?"

"Yes," I said.

"Yes." Jason nodded.

"Well…er…um…Miss Tanaka, do you want this job?" Before she could respond, he asked, "What is the job, by the way?"

"Being a nanny to our…my sister's baby."

"Oh, Sasumi will be perfect for that." The woman patted the young woman's delicate, pale hand then the family took off.

"Well, I guess you'll be needing this." The desk sergeant handed her the gas mask the family had just turned in.

Sasumi took it and looked at the ground.

"What were you going to do if they left you here?" I asked her.

Sasumi didn't seem especially thrilled to have a new job. "I do not know."

"There are a lot of Japanese people without work." The desk sergeant shrugged. "The Fosters really did mean to be kind. They're just anxious to get home."

"Well, she has work now. And a home." I patted Sasumi's arm and she followed me and Jason outside.

"Tinder," the desk sergeant shrieked. I turned. He held up my gas mask. "Don't forget this."

I snatched it out of his hand. I'd forgotten I'd even put it on his counter.

Sheesh.

* * * *

Sasumi followed us into the studio as Jason rounded up a couple of his friends to load up a borrowed truck with as much stuff as we could manage.

"We'll come back," he said, peeling off five-dollar notes for all those who'd helped us. I drove the car, with the baby and Sasumi and a ton of our belongings packed into the back seat and trunk.

Jason followed us in the truck. At the house, we unloaded everything inside and I set about mixing the baby's formula before he started crying.

"I can do it," Sasumi said.

With some of our kitchen supplies with us, I was able to offer her a cup of green tea. She seemed surprised, but eagerly accepted my offer.

"Mrs Foster would never make me tea."

"Well, you don't know Tinder yet, but you'll soon find out how wonderful he is." Jason smiled at her. To me he said, "Sweetheart, I'll go back and grab more stuff. You stay here with the baby and Sasumi. I'll be back as fast as I can." He gave me a swift kiss, then realised Sasumi was watching us. She looked shocked. Then she started to giggle.

"You explain things to her," Jason said.

"I think we just did."

Sasumi stopped giggling when Jason left. She seemed nervous again. Her gaze dropped. She seemed suddenly frightened. I worried that maybe the shock of two men kissing had disgusted her.

"Are you...tired?" I asked her.

"A little." Her head came up.

"You didn't sleep well, I'll bet. I can't imagine what it feels like to be you, Sasumi. Where is your family?"

"There is only my father. I miss him sometimes. He is in San Francisco." She lapsed into silence.

I boiled the water and moved around the kitchen, unpacking things we'd hastily thrown into boxes and bags. I watched her feeding the baby and liked the tender way she handled him.

I looked around at the cupboards, trying to decide where to store our glassware and dishes. We'd packed with such speed it surprised me that nothing was broken. Dumb luck, I supposed.

Music. We needed some nice, relaxing music. More than anything, I was pleased to have the radio in the house. Jason and I had missed it even for just one morning. I noticed Sasumi kept turning in her chair to watch me as I organised things. She seemed so intrigued by me. I turned on the radio and The Andrew Sisters began singing *Bounce Me Brother*. I sang and danced along with it. Sasumi laughed and laughed.

"I told my father that my reputation for being the class clown would pay off one day," I told her.

Over tea, I held the baby, who didn't seem inclined to sleep. He was as fascinated by the dark-haired beauty as I was. I asked Sasumi about her life. She was a Nisei, the first generation of American-Japanese children born to a family in San Francisco. Her father had worked the goldfields of Northern California and the sugar fields of Hawaii as a contract worker. He'd worked off his contract then returned to California a free man. She said he'd been given a lot of money by his former boss in exchange for fulfilling his commitment to him, and then started his own business.

"Your father must be a very strong man, a good man. I know a few Nisei whose fathers worked so hard. Working off those contracts though...that's almost impossible."

"Hai." Her cheeks flushed. "Yes." She'd started to open up by the time we started eating mooncakes. Mooncakes will do that to a person.

Sasumi said her father believed in hard work and, after her mother died four years ago, had sent her to Honolulu to go to college and pay her way with a job. It seemed an incredibly unusual and challenging thing for him to do for his daughter. Then she casually mentioned it was her stepmother's idea and I understood. The new wife wanted her out of the way.

Her father and stepmother had met a woman who said Sasumi could work in the 'exciting' new Hawaiian travel industry, make big money and go to college. Sasumi had been so happy to experience the islands her father had told her about. The only problem was that the woman who had brought her and twelve other girls here from California had not been honest with Sasumi's father or the other parents. She had intended to use Sasumi as a prostitute exclusively for Japanese businessmen.

"A comfort woman," I said, for I knew the Japanese called the women that.

Sasumi nodded, clearly still devastated.

"Were you forced to work?"

She hung her head. "Yes." She blinked. "And then I ran away."

"Good for you." I put the baby on my shoulder and stroked his back. "Did anybody hurt you, Sasumi?"

She shook her head.

That was a relief. But I understood why she hadn't gone home again. She had been ashamed. Sasumi said that she had managed to get away from the woman, who took what little money the girl had. Sasumi had found work through the Schofield Barracks Society as a nanny. Her most recent position had been for a year. The Foster family she'd worked for liked her to wear traditional garb, but she said on the mainland she dressed like everybody else.

"How do you want to dress here?" I asked her.

She hung her head. "I only have kimonos. I have nothing else. They...Mrs Foster threw everything I owned away."

I certainly didn't want her dressing in a style that made her uncomfortable but had no idea how to find her new things. *Wait... I did* know. Liberty House. She also had no money. The Fosters had paid her almost nothing. Their meagre payments had trickled to a big, fat zero when Pearl Harbor was attacked, yet, from what I understood, she had continued to work all day long.

That meant we'd have to buy her some things. We could manage that. I was surprised to learn Sasumi was twenty-two and had never even owned her own bank account. When Jason came home, I told him her story. We packed up her and the baby and took them to Chinatown to the bank. Jason helped her open a savings account. I noticed the shocked expression on Jiao's face.

As for Sasumi, she studied her little blue savings book as if it were her ticket to freedom. In fact...it was. Jason put some money into her account and told her she could come in whenever she needed to add or withdraw money. She would earn a weekly salary to do with as she wished. We would pay her each Friday and if she wished to put money into her account, she could. If she wanted to buy things, that was her choice.

She listened intently then whispered *choice* as if it were an unfamiliar word.

Sasumi was fascinated by the bank. I had a feeling, in the future, she might just want to work here.

Jiao didn't leave us alone for a second. When the baby fussed and Sasumi held him, Jiao's jaw actually dropped.

Clutching her passbook in her hands, Sasumi gently put the baby in his pram and the three of us left the bank. She was very deferential to Jiao, who quirked a brow when Sasumi bowed slightly to her.

We drove back to Waikiki and went to Liberty House. Sasumi sat in the back with the baby, which was fine by me. He was safer in the back seat and I wanted him to get used to her.

At Liberty House, Sasumi loved the store but something strange happened when she met my father. They stood, staring at one another, transfixed.

"Do you see what I see?" Jason asked as my father organised a female assistant to help Sasumi pick out some new clothes. "Your dad's got a little crush."

My father's assistant came running. Dad was needed in the shipping office. He retreated and Sasumi snapped out of her haze. She seemed so happy with the three dresses she tried on. I thought they were very plain, but pretty things seemed to have vanished overnight in Waikiki. We bought her the dresses and two pairs of flat shoes. I asked her in a low voice if she needed underwear.

She giggled. "No."

"You must bring her to the house tomorrow," my father said as we were leaving.

"Tomorrow?"

"The meeting…remember?"

No, I'd forgotten.

Jason dropped us off at home, planning to make one more run to Chinatown. "I think one more truckload is all we have in the place," he said.

I kissed him. "Don't be long."

He touched my cheek. "I won't. I already miss you, babe."

I helped Sasumi get her bedroom prepared. I hadn't had time to clean it before, but as the baby slept, Sasumi and I threw ourselves into the effort. I removed Melody's few things, packed them in the suitcase from her wardrobe and put it in the linen closet. I put clean sheets on her bed. I showed Sasumi the bathroom that would be for her personal use and gave her clean towels.

She burst into tears and dropped at my feet.

"Oh, my God, Sasumi, don't do that." I rushed to help her get up again.

"You are so kind," she said. "You are so very kind." She seemed so emotional and so lonely. "I can't go home. After everything my father went through...they will take him away!"

I felt awful for her. I got the feeling dressing like a geisha girl was only the beginning of her bad experiences with her previous employers. Hunting around for something to bring a smile to her face, I found a Crosley turntable I'd bought at a yard sale.

"Keep this in your room," I said. I'd picked up a couple of records with it, almost brand new. One was the Tommy Dorsey Orchestra with Frank Sinatra, the other was my favourite gals, The Andrews Sisters.

Sasumi was overwhelmed. "For me?" You might have thought I'd given her diamonds.

After leaving her alone to get changed, I finished getting the house looking beautiful. I was excited to be in the big, new house and when Jason came home with the rest of our things, I ran to the door, ready to throw myself into his arms.

Two big men stood behind him. Men in uniform.

Oops.

Jason smiled. Thank God I hadn't actually mauled him. He quickly introduced the two men as being officers from the Military Government. I turned off the radio.

"We just moved in," I said. "I'm sorry, we're still in a bit of a mess."

"Not a problem," the first one said. They sat on the sofa. I had a horrible thought that Jason might have left the K-Y Jelly there and I hoped it wouldn't suddenly resurface.

Jason and I grabbed the first two chairs we could find and sat across from them.

"What's going on?" I asked, wondering if being blunt might be a mistake.

Jason turned to me. "Officers Jones and Carmody told me that Melody was sent home because she violated the rules for being here. Apparently she registered as a working girl and broke some of the rules straight away."

I stared at Jason, wondering what the hell was *really* going on. Which one was Jones and which one was Carmody? They were both the most humourless men I'd ever met.

"So, she is okay?" I asked.

"Yes," one of the officers said. I hadn't taken in either man's name and kept kicking myself mentally. I stared at Jason. I was trying to figure out why they were here and exactly what I was supposed to say.

"As I mentioned before, Melody was somebody we met before the war," Jason said to the two men. His tone was a little artificial. I could hear the stress in his voice. "Tinder and Melody knew each other from going to the same doctor, and when she left the islands, he never expected to see her again."

"When *was* the last time you saw her?" one of the men asked me.

"Before Pearl Harbor was attacked. She left the islands. She said she was going to San Francisco. I never saw her again." I glanced at Jason who gave me a slight nod. "I was told by a mutual friend in Chinatown a couple of days ago that she was back, but seemed to have disappeared. I didn't actually see her myself."

"Yes, it's very strange," one of the men said. "She came here as the wife of an officer, but then registered as a..."—his face coloured as he fumbled for the right words—"sex worker, which is really against all the rules. From what we understand, the officer felt...compromised because he hadn't known about her past."

I felt terrible for Melody. She would never be allowed to forget her past. I was lucky mine didn't crop up more often, but then I hadn't slept with any high-ranking officials and, in comparison with female sex workers, very few sailors and soldiers.

"She was given permission to work because she needed money and we needed the girls. She appealed directly to the Provost Marshal and promised to follow the rules."

"Which she didn't," the other officer chimed in. "She violated the first rule. She was seen in the company of another officer at a restaurant. This is strictly prohibited."

"I see." I remembered this rule. There were so many unofficial commandments for the working girls of Honolulu. I wondered who the hell had reported Melody, considering that she hadn't been working for an actual madam, but had gone into business with Jean O'Hara.

"So you never saw her at all when she returned?" the first officer asked.

I shook my head. "No, never. I became concerned because other people were worried. She just seemed to have disappeared."

"She was caught in a raid with Jean O'Hara and another woman right in this very house."

Both men stared at me. I thought I would die on the spot. I was so shocked they came right out with it.

I stared at Jason who looked back at me. I couldn't read his expression.

"Somebody mentioned it to us in Chinatown. Jason and I came here hoping to find her and we saw Jean

O'Hara. I had never met her before. I don't think it's a secret that she was beaten badly in that raid you mentioned."

The men exchanged glances. "No, it's not," one of the officers said. "She has told a number of people and filed a complaint with the Police Commissioner."

Oh, great. Gabrielson hates her and now she's gone...

"She was in a lot of pain," I said. "We took her to the dentist. You should have seen her. She was a mess. He said her injuries were severe so we took her to the hospital."

"Where is she now?"

"I have no idea. We picked her up again. We brought her back here but she said she wanted to get away, wanted to sell the house." I looked at Jason. He needed to help me out here. I was sweating in my shoes. I certainly wasn't going to tell them we almost helped smuggle her to Maui. For all we knew, she was still on Oahu.

Jason nodded. "As I explained to these two officers when they came to my office, we bought the house from Jean, but we hadn't known her until yesterday."

"Right," I said. "I'd never met her before." That was the truth. I was starting to follow things now. He'd been ambushed. The police must have been keeping an eye on Jean and had passed on the information to the military government. They had found out awfully quickly that we'd bought her house. How had that happened?

Jiao. It came to me in an instant.

Should we mention Christopher? I waited for Jason's lead.

"And you bought this house together?" one of the officers asked.

I smiled. "Yes. We've begun a new partnership. Did you tell them, Jason?"

He nodded. "We're planning a new development next door. The loan application came to my desk and I'm interested in taking over the project. Tinder is an architect and we like the idea of providing wonderful accommodations for our military personnel arriving in the islands."

I could see Jason was sweating, too.

Sasumi chose that moment to enter the room. She immediately shrank back.

"Am I interrupting?"

"No," Jason said, introducing her. "Sasumi started working for us today."

"Yes," one of them said. "We know. As a nanny to your sister's baby."

My blood chilled. Boy, there were few secrets on the island. Did they know I didn't have a sister?

I glanced back at the men. They were too busy ogling Sasumi. I could tell they found her attractive. In her regular clothing, Sasumi looked like a modest, unassuming young woman. I felt very protective of her all of a sudden. I was glad we'd bought her some new clothes, even if they were a little...dowdy. Her kimono might have been very awkward to explain. I shuddered inwardly, thinking how it might have looked had she been wearing a kimono. They might have thought the brothel was in full swing.

"Can we offer you some tea or coffee?" I asked. "I'm sorry, I should have offered sooner."

"No," the first officer said, rising to his feet. "We have everything we need."

The other man stood. They seemed to be taking everything in.

"How do you like your radio?" the first officer asked, gesturing at our Crosley.

"We love it," I said.

"I have one, too." He smiled at me for the first time. "I look forward to seeing your new houses."

We shook hands with both men. When they left, Jason gripped my shoulders.

"Well done."

I hugged him quickly and we turned to Sasumi, who looked from one to the other of us.

"Those men frightened me," she said.

"Me, too," I told her. She giggled as if that was the funniest thing she'd ever heard.

Jason and I exchanged looks. He inclined his head and we excused ourselves.

In our bedroom, we shut the door. He checked on the baby then took me in his arms, his lips finding mine in the perfect kiss.

He cupped my face in his hands. "Tinder...they didn't mention it here but they told me Melody was given the choice of jail time—"

"Jail time!"

He nodded. "Or immediate passage out of here. She pissed off somebody very important."

"The guy we saw in the car?"

"Maybe. What I believe is that she chose to leave. She was told she had to leave right away. I don't think she took anything."

"But she left some things."

"Yeah. Things the other two didn't want. The other girl took off. Her room was stripped bare. Who's to say they both didn't cherry-pick through her things?"

"But what about the baby? How could she leave him? I could *never* do that to a child."

"Baby, I don't think she had much of a choice, but I agree with you—she should have taken him, too. I suspect she hoped right until the end that her mucky-muck would change his mind and beg her to stay."

"So you think when she went to see Mrs Chan, it was to tell her to find us?"

"I think so. I don't think she gave her much information...maybe something like, 'If I don't come back, find Tinder'."

I thought for a minute. It made sense that her brief visit with the old lady was a stop on the way to the ship. She'd asked the caretaker to find me. I still thought her actions were wrong. I would never have left my child.

Jason seemed to be reading my thoughts. "She knew you would take care of him. Who knows...she may reach out to us and ask for us to send him back to her."

"Oh, Jason. It's so wrong...like he doesn't even exist. Nobody's asked about him. We're threatened not to mention him and—"

"Nobody wants him but us. If she ever comes after him, we'll deal with it. But I'm not prepared to give him up without a fight."

"God, I love you."

He gave me a wonderful smile. We began to kiss, falling on the bed. With curfew coming soon, we didn't have much time. We didn't want Sasumi all alone in the living room, but we were soon reaching for one another's zipper. We grabbed each other's cock and began to suck. I'd never been into this style of mutual pleasuring until I met Jason. Now I loved it. We matched each other's rhythm—a little lick, a kiss, a little sucking, some licking... Soon, we were all over each other. We sucked each other until we both came.

He held my ass in both his hands as my cock tore down his throat.

Jason turned himself around so that we were facing each other. Sometimes I loved those fast and thirsty cock-sucks.

"I want more later," he said, kissing me.

In the kitchen, we found to our astonishment that Sasumi had done a good job of checking the house for blackened windows and had even prepared dinner – stir-fried chicken, rice and vegetables.

She'd even found our sake and heated the drink. She poured us each a cup.

We sat in semi-darkness around the coffee table. Her food was delicious.

"The Fosters always kept their lights on," Sasumi remarked. "They kept flashlights in every room, in case the air wardens caught them."

We didn't say anything. We weren't the Fosters and our situation was different. We were two men who slept together. We tried to draw as little attention to ourselves as possible. Nobody was supposed to use lights at night. We knew that some people did. Besides, we liked candlelight and thought of it as more romantic.

"I like to cook," she said. "When Christopher is older, I can make food for him, too."

"Sasumi," Jason said, "You do know we are a couple, don't you?"

She smiled, putting her chopsticks across her bowl and giggled, hand over her mouth. "Yes."

"Are you okay with this?" Jason asked. I loved the deft way he handled chopsticks. He could pick up a single grain of rice and swallow it. He shovelled food into his mouth faster, as if he were afraid of her answer.

"Do you love each other?" she asked.

"Very much," Jason said, mouth full.

"Then I am very okay with it."

We all smiled at each other. Jason picked up his sake cup and toasted the two of us.

"To our new little family," he said.

"Hai!" Sasumi said. We clicked sake cups and drank.

Less than an hour later, Jason and I were in bed together, naked and cuddling. It had been another long day and we fell into a sweet sleep. He began to have nightmares and I held him tight. I stroked his back and comforted him, rocking him back to sleep. And then my other baby began to wail. I got out of bed and started the process all over again. As I gazed at my two darlings, however, I knew I would willingly lose sleep, in the name of love. Each and every day. I watched Jason's beautiful face, no longer troubled now he was dreaming of prettier things.

And in that dark hour, under a quiet Hawaiian sky, I was glad my abiding heart had chosen him to love.

Chapter Five

Exactly eighteen men showed up to my father's meeting. He seemed happy, though. The group leader, a Mr Richard C. Tong, was in the middle of combat training and there was a ripple of excitement at the mention of those words. "Six more people here than last week," he announced.

My father spoke next. "Please, everybody, invite your friends. There is a new volunteer corps just formed in Kauai made up entirely of Filipino plantation workers. Their islands are, after all, being occupied by the Japanese."

"I'm Japanese," one of the men blurted. "And I did not invade the Philippines!"

My father held up his hand. "I didn't say you did, Mr Hagaki. Besides, you are Japanese-Hawaiian. There's a big difference."

This seemed to mollify Mr Hagaki who settled down after his outburst.

"Now," my father said, "the Military Governor, Mr Emmons, is encouraging all volunteer efforts. As soon as we have more members, we can start training, but he has mentioned to me the biggest problem facing the island right now is a critical shortage of air wardens."

He scanned the page in his hand. "Civilian Governor Mr Poindexter has sent me a note saying that the women of our island are becoming air wardens, too. As a matter of fact, my wife, Linda, is the new air warden in our neighbourhood."

A murmur went up in the group. My thoughts raced to the dual governors. Under Martial Law, every executive post in the islands had a military shadow. With the goal of the islands' safety in mind, there had been surprisingly little public scuffling. But behind the scenes, who knew?

"What would we have to do exactly?" Mr Hagaki asked.

My father said the air wardens were responsible for patrolling their district for blackout violations and keeping an eye out for other problems.

"I could do that!" a couple of men said. The meeting went on. I wondered how Sasumi was getting along with Linda in the kitchen. I excused myself. Jason shot me an inquisitive look. I mouthed, "*Sasumi*," and he nodded.

In the kitchen, I was surprised to find Sasumi standing on her toes, bent over the sink, Linda scrubbing her head with soap.

The baby was asleep in his pram. To my horror, I saw that he had a Bible tucked into it. I gritted my teeth.

"What's going on?" I asked.

"I'm washing her hair. Do you know this lacquer is impossible to get out?"

"No, I didn't know."

"Tinder, take the coffee into the living room. I borrowed an urn from one of my neighbours. There should be enough for everybody."

"Sure thing," I said. I was so surprised that Linda was doing something nice for somebody else that I impulsively hugged her from behind.

"What's that for?"

"Thank you for being kind to Sasumi."

"I'm doing it for her. Not for you." Her smile, however, showed me she was pleased with my compliment.

We stayed for lunch and I was happy that Linda seemed to be a little nicer to the baby. Sasumi and I took care of his feeding and diaper changing, but Linda rocked his pram a couple of times.

My father talked to me and Jason about Christopher.

"If she really did sail back to San Francisco, I can try and trace her through my shipping connections," he said. "Like you, it worries me that she would just abandon him. It doesn't seem…likely, but I don't know the woman. Who knows what measures desperate people take?"

I had no answer for that. We just didn't know. In the afternoon, we dropped Sasumi and the baby off at home then Jason and I drove into Chinatown. We had trouble finding parking, with volunteer training sessions taking place in the grounds of 'Iolani Palace and the park surrounding it. We walked down to Chinatown itself, finding it difficult to get past the swarms of uniformed men looking for a good time. We checked on the laundries and dry cleaners. They were doing fine, however it was difficult for people to get quick delivery of their clean clothes. Every washing machine was in use from sunrise to sunset. One of the women pointed to the long line of bags filled with clothing waiting to be cleaned. There wasn't much we could do about that.

"It would be great if we could let people wash the clothes themselves," Jason said as we walked down the street. "You know, they could rent the machines."

"That's a great idea," I responded.

On the corner of River Street overlooking the river itself, some Chinese families had set up camp selling off their possessions. As usual, we perused everything. Jason suddenly frowned.

"Tinder...this is my office furniture!"

We were stunned. He knew his office better than anyone. I could tell he was devastated. He started asking the sellers questions. He turned to me, barely masking his fury.

"Jiao's family gave it to them. Can you believe that? She took my furniture!"

He offered the family cash for his most prized pieces and we started carrying things down to the bank. A couple of sailors pitched in and helped. We gave them six dollars each. That would get them a hooker and a tattoo, or a hooker and fake gin, whichever they preferred.

"Why does the gin here taste so funny?" one of them asked us.

"Because it's made locally and it's nothing like the gin from the mainland," I told them. They looked horrified.

"But it's in bottles from the mainland."

I shook my head. "Mainland gin is scarce and those bottles are now being recycled and packaged out of plants here on the island."

"That's…just wrong!"

"That's the result of war," Jason responded.

The bank was closed as it was Saturday. Jason unlocked the doors. We thanked our helpers, taking in everything ourselves then locking up behind us.

Jason's office door was open. To our amazement, we heard a voice.

I could hear Jiao talking on the phone.

"He is hardly ever here," she said. "He is so busy with the war effort. He and that *friend* of his. No, I don't know where the combination to the safe is, but I know he has lots of money—"

She gasped when she looked up and saw us standing there.

"Who are you talking to, Jiao?" Jason asked, his eyes icy little slits.

"Nobody." She quickly hung up.

"You have two choices." Jason's voice was even and quiet. I'd never heard such contained anger in him before. "You can tell me what's been going on here or I'll have you arrested for theft."

She gaped at him. "Theft?"

"You stole all my office furniture. We just bought it back."

She glanced from left to right.

"I can explain."

"Go on. Explain." He stood, arms folded, right in front of her.

"I didn't think you'd be back for a long time and I—I didn't like your furniture. I gave it to my father."

"You didn't like my furniture? What does that have to do with you? I didn't leave my business in your hands. I'm calling the police."

"The war office." She seemed suddenly frantic. "Ever since you came back, they've been asking me questions. I know Harumi and Sheido were supposed to look after things when you were away, but it was me. I took over. Then you came back and the war office wanted to know if you are…" Her voice fell away.

"What?" he prompted. "They want to know if I am…what?"

"An enemy or a friend of Hawaii."

We gaped at her.

"Who were you talking to just now?" he asked again. She sank back, miserable.

"Somebody in Governor Emmons' office."

"Who?"

"His secretary. He calls me every day." Jiao was defiant. "I never told them anything that wasn't true."

Jason picked up the phone and called the Governor's office.

"Wait outside," he said to Jiao. She scurried out like a petrified rabbit. I closed the door behind her, as Jason took possession of his office chair. He looked ashen as he began to talk to whomever was on the other end of the line. I sat opposite him, watching, waiting. I had a feeling that Jiao was just on the other side of the door. When I opened it, she almost fell into the room.

"You're fired, Jiao," Jason said. "I have discussed this matter with the Governor's office. They said you called them first to offer them information. In case you haven't seen the street signs, Jiao, gossiping and spreading rumours is now against the law in these islands."

"But—"

"You are dismissed. Give me your keys."

She became an instant wreck. "This bank is my whole life."

"Not anymore."

He took her key and escorted her outside. When he returned, I put my arms around him, but he pushed me away.

"I can't hold you when I feel like this. I can't poison our sweetness with this bitterness."

"Yes, you can," I insisted. I held him and heard his heart beating so fast that I worried he would have a heart attack.

"I've done everything, spread myself so thin. I've tried everything to prove my loyalty. Tinder, I'm very worried about this tribunal."

"You're going to be fine," I said.

"I want you there."

"Then I will be there." His heartbeat slowed as I stroked his back and he finally lifted his face from my shoulder.

"Tinder, I just want to walk away from everything."

"I understand."

I took control and pushed all of his furniture back into his office. We locked up and walked to the car. I knew how to make him feel better. I drove over the Pali Highway and after squeezing around truckloads of new recruits coming and going from Army manoeuvres, we drove down to Kailua Beach. Jason grinned as we kicked off our shoes and ran to the water, dropping everything but our underpants. There was no barbed wire on this side of the island. Farther along the coast, closer to Waimanalo, there was barbed wire since it was close to some of the military bases.

We swam and frolicked in the ocean. The water felt frothy and cold, its colour a brilliant blue. Out in the distance we saw battle ships emerging on the horizon, a reminder of the true state of things.

"God, I want to fuck you," Jason said, his hand on my butt cheek as we stole back on to the sand.

I didn't think it was a good idea but said, "I want you, too." He had that look in his eye. He needed and wanted me and I never, ever denied him. I almost caved in and looked for a private spot, but two soldiers had just arrived, towels over their shoulders. Thank God we hadn't done anything stupid. We greeted them. They remarked on how inviting the water looked. We told them, almost in unison, "The water is great," as we threw on our clothes. We almost ran to the car, Jason grinning at me.

"You know, I wonder what they would have done if they'd found me fucking you."

"Let's not think about that." I didn't think being jailed was an experience either of us needed.

* * * *

Monday, January 26, 1942

My father sat, staring with a look of smug satisfaction at his hand of poker. We were playing cards with him and a couple of his neighbours, including Mr Hagaki, who turned out to be a pretty good player. His son, who was also supposed to be playing, kept staring at Sasumi, who seemed oblivious.

We'd just had a fantastic meal of Chicken Divan. It was a recipe Linda had found in a dog-eared copy of *Everywoman* magazine from the previous September. She showed us the cover that featured an article called 'The Cut-Down Dress'. A little girl was depicted standing on a stool in an over-sized dress as her mother measured and pinned it to make it smaller. To me, the little girl looked glum.

"This magazine's been circulating the neighbourhood. I can make extra money cutting down old dresses for little girls!" Linda said.

"Are you in?" my father asked me. I'd almost forgotten I was playing poker. But judging by his smug expression, I knew he had a good hand.

"I'm out," I said, laying down my cards.

I was glad Linda had found a passion for something other than exhorting the Bible. I considered myself a Christian man but Linda had, since I'd met her, veered from being normal, to being the victim of her own Bible-belting family beating her for marrying my father, then to thinking that Christopher was possessed by the devil. Sewing seemed a harmless and perhaps profitable pursuit.

"We could set you up in business," Jason said. How like my man.

"You would do that?" Linda's eyes grew dreamy.

"I would like to help!"

Sasumi sounded so eager and Linda said, "We can make you some new clothes that way."

"You could make me a shirt," Mr Hagaki's son said. He turned beet red when all eyes turned on him.

Sasumi had already told me and Jason that she was anxious to prove her loyalty to the government. She said she wanted to be the air warden for our neighbourhood.

"I'll help you," Linda said. I was pleased to see Linda taking Sasumi under her wing.

That night, we were to sleep on the floor of the living room. We didn't mind. Sasumi and the baby were in the guest room. When the neighbours slipped back next door, my father turned to me and Jason.

My father sat opposite us on the sofa, his face grave.

"Jason, you know you have to give testimony in a few days."

"Yes." Of course he knew.

"Do you want to go over some things here...just between us?"

Jason almost came unglued. "No."

"You really should practice."

Jason looked at him, blinking through tears. "I don't have the strength to tell it too many times." His face crumpled in grief. "They hurt me, Dad."

My father's eyes moistened. Jason had never called him Dad before. Something had shifted between them.

"I know, son, I know." He put his arms around my man. "I won't let anyone hurt you again. I will be there with you."

I put my arms around the two men I loved most in this world. All three of us wept.

* * * *

Wednesday, January 28, 1942

Jason and I walked into the military tribunal, which would take place in the throne room of 'Iolani Palace. A dozen military officers swirled around as we waited to be called into the meeting. A lot of rooms had been closed off and had signs posted saying *Classified! Authorised Personnel Only.* Jason was nervous. We all were. The tribunal consisted of four American military leaders, a military police officer, and a British Naval Officer who would incorporate the findings of this tribunal along with other mounting reports of Japanese military atrocities to the British Parliament.

Along the left wall was a credenza. We put our gas masks on it. I noticed a pitcher of water with several glasses on it. I was going to ask Jason if he wanted some water, but the meeting had already started. The tribunal members sat at a long table, Jason in a chair opposite them. There was another chair beside him, empty.

I wanted to sit beside him, but my father shook his head and patted the seat next to him, on the other side of the room.

My father moved beside Jason and spoke first, saying that he had known the Qui family for many years and that in his experience they had always been very fair and honourable businessmen.

"Jason is like a son to me," my father said. "He and my own son Tinder are the best of friends. When Jason wanted to join the cargo ship, the SS *Malama*, we wanted to support him. We were devastated when we discovered the ship had been attacked and the crew captured."

My father swallowed and cleared his throat. I had never seen him so emotional. "I am ashamed to admit that when certain sources gave my son information about Jason's escape and informed him that he and two others were on Kahao'olawe, I discouraged him from acting. Not because I wanted to abandon Jason, but because I was afraid it was a trap. I was afraid that these people only wanted whatever money my son was willing to give them. I truly did not believe Jason had escaped."

This was an admission that surprised me. It also made sense. I realised now how foolish and headstrong I must have seemed. I also realised my father understood the depth of my feelings for the man I loved and that was really why he was here.

My mother would have been proud.

Dad moved away again and my heart went out to Jason, who looked so small and so alone.

"Go on, son," the leader of the tribunal said to Jason. His tone wasn't unkind, but not exactly encouraging, either. "Take your time and, in your own words, tell us what happened."

Jason glanced at me, then flattened his palms on his thighs. He looked away from the men at the table and looked at my father.

To my surprise, my father stood and moved back beside Jason. I dared not move, lest the magical moment be ruined. Jason knew I was there. Having my father beside him would give him the strength he needed.

"We set out in the early morning of December twenty-sixth." His voice sounded determined. That was a good sign.

"Did you volunteer for this mission or were you asked to take part in it?" the British Officer asked.

"No, I did not volunteer. For the record, my family owns a prominent bank in Chinatown and I have frequently travelled on cargo ships to mainland China and to Hong Kong on company business. I was approached after it became obvious that my uncle had stolen money from some of our investors. I was in the process of replacing all these funds when I was approached about the mission to the Philippines."

Jason took a deep breath. "I didn't feel pressured to take the assignment, but I did feel…obligated."

"Who asked you to take the assignment?" the British Officer asked. The three men beside him gave him such furious looks he seemed to shrink into himself.

"I believe, from the letter I received, that this is classified information and that I am not at liberty to —"

"Go on," said the first man. "What was your mission, as you understood it?"

"I understood the mission was to take a secret radar set-up to the Philippines."

"Why did they ask you when you're not in the military?" the British Officer asked.

"I suppose because I'm expendable."

The shockwaves of Jason's honesty seemed to rattle the tribunal officials.

"There were military officers on board, also merchant seamen. They seemed very excited about the voyage. My job was to let the Philippine government know that they were not isolated, that they were valuable to the war effort."

He looked at me and I knew he wanted water. I moved swiftly to the sideboard and poured him a glass. When I handed it to him, his eyes looked flat and frightened.

Jason took a long draught and resumed his story. "We all believed in our mission." He looked up, eyeing every man on the other side of the table. He repeated his words. He wanted to make sure they understood.

"At the dockyard, I heard another Matson cargo ship had been bombed. We knew the risk we were taking but we believed that our lives were worth less than the task ahead, to take the radar set-up to the Philippines."

None of the men said anything. They were riveted.

"On January first, Japanese sea planes arrived overhead. It happened so fast. They started dropping incendiary bombs and hundred-pounders." He shook his head. "We had no idea they'd been tracking us. I admit I've never been so scared in my life. Captain Peters, the captain of our ship, made a split-second decision. He didn't want the radar getting into enemy hands. We all helped to toss it overboard. Then he was yelling at us to jump overboard into the ship's lifeboats. The Japanese pilots were shouting at us to surrender. The whole time, they kept firing at us."

He took another drink.

"We all went overboard as the ship went down." He paused. "And then they started capturing us." He swallowed again and the glass tipped in his shaking hand. I was still standing. I'd been so mesmerised by his tale that I'd forgotten to sit down. I moved over to him to take the glass away. He shook his head. He wanted more and I refilled it for him.

This time I sat as Jason resumed his story. "The raiders arrived and started surrounding us. For such huge vessels, they moved fast. I feel stupid admitting this but I hadn't noticed them before. I was in a lifeboat with three other men. Their sea planes kept flying so close to us that we couldn't escape. We were captured when one of the raiders came right beside us and shot at us. There were two of them. The *Aikoku Maru* and *Haikoku Maru*. The sea planes came from those raiders. They shot at us and…we went overboard. We kept trying to stay underwater so they couldn't take us."

Jason looked at my father. "I don't know how we survived."

My father put his arm around his shoulders. I fought off tears. I had to be strong for Jason. I tried to keep my face impassive especially since I knew we were just hearing the beginning of his story.

"The lifeboat went down. I'd been hiding under it, but it started to sink. One of the merchant seamen told me later that it takes a lot to sink a lifeboat. Well, it sank. I came up for breath and got hit on the head from behind. I remember going down and I thought I would drown. I was so surprised when I woke up and I was on board the *Aikoku Maru*. It was a big vessel and a lot of the crew from the SS *Malama* was on there. We were on the deck, tied up with ropes like a bunch of sardines.

"It was getting dark and—"

"Did you know where you were when the SS *Malama* was attacked?"

"Oh, yes. We were heading towards Tahiti. I didn't know where we were at that point, though. A lot of time had passed. I could hear the Japanese crew talking. I pretended to still be unconscious. I could hear them and I do speak some Japanese because of my business dealings, but when I heard their plans for us, I knew I had to escape."

"What plans?" one of the officers asked.

"They were going to take us to Woo Sung Prisoner of War Camp."

"Woo Sung?" The men all began to speak at once. It was obvious they'd never heard of it.

"I heard them say it's in China. They couldn't *wait* to torture us. I couldn't let them take me to the land of my family and *torture* me."

"So what did you do?"

"They came for me and a few of the others. They took us below deck to a galley. I watched them raping the youngest crew member. It was awful. He was so young and he was crying and they kept hitting him and punching him as they took turns abusing him." He dropped his head and began to cry.

The officers were stunned silent.

"They all kept smiling. That's what I remember. They took turns raping us and they thought it was funny."

I went rigid. *They raped Jason?*

"They used these special paddles to beat us as they raped us. It was worse for the Americans, though—the actual military. The Japanese crew seemed intent on humiliating and punishing them the most."

Jason stared at his hands as they seemed to rub at the pleat in his pants of their own volition. I stared at him. How would he ever forget these memories? I recalled the way he'd wanted me to fuck him when he came home. He'd winced in pain…but he wanted me inside him. He wanted good feelings after the bad. I'd had no idea what he had endured.

"And they raped you?" the British officer asked.

"Yes. One of them did, but they kept attacking the poor sailor. He was sobbing. Blood was coming out of him but they kept raping him. They punched him in the mouth. They broke his teeth. He begged them to kill him."

Jason's head drooped.

"They took him away. I heard a gunshot. Maybe they killed him, but I don't know. I do know they started to worry then because they marched us back up to the deck. I think the officers who'd abused us got into trouble. Not because they abused us but because they were supposed to let the torture linger." He paused. "That's why I believe they shot that poor sailor.

"They forced the rest of us to get into these cargo cages. Mine didn't lock properly. They had no idea. The two men Tinder found with me were in the cage, too. There was a fourth man but he refused to allow us to talk him into escaping. He was very scared."

"How did you escape?" I asked, forgetting where I was for a moment.

"When they put us in the cages, they suddenly had an emergency. Some problem with one of their gas units. They were afraid the whole raider would blow up so they were all running around dealing with that. It was dark and confused. For me, it seemed like perfect timing, so the three of us got out of the cage, stole over the side of the raider and cut loose one of their lifeboats."

I was so proud of him. He drained his glass. The four men sitting opposite him seemed stunned.

"Do you know who the sailor was?" one of the officers asked.

Jason shook his head. "I feel bad about him every single day."

"How did you get to Kaho'olawe?"

Jason looked at them, relief flooding his eyes. "A Tahitian fisherman. Can you believe it? He had a huge fishing boat and he took us. I fell asleep. I was in a lot of pain from the beating I took. I peed blood into the ocean. I felt pretty sick. He seemed anxious to help. He took us to one of the outer islands and, from there, another boat—a small cargo ship that came from the Marquesas group—brought us close to Hawaii. They ran into a fishing trawler and dropped us off. The crew there took us to Kaho'olawe. They were afraid to take us to Maui. Even out at sea, rumours of Japanese invasion frighten people.

"Kaho'lawe is abandoned, as you know, so they felt safe leaving us there. They said they would make contact with friends in Honolulu and let them know we'd survived."

It was my turn to talk next, but they didn't seem very interested in my story. I told them an anonymous fisherman approached me in Chinatown and told me that Jason was on Kaho'olawe. I did not mention that this news came via my former brothel madam.

They did tell me I was a good friend and a brave soul and after they asked Jason a few more questions they let us go. We went to grab all of our gas masks. *Unbelievable.* Mine was missing.

Outside the palace, Jason looked pale.

"I need to go home," he said. "I think I'm going to throw up."

* * * *

Jason was a lot better later that afternoon. He slept in our bed after I gave him mint tea and sliced melon. He awoke from a fitful nap and I pushed the big radio into our room so we could listen to music. He smiled when I brought the baby in to greet him. Our little guy was doing great and he made such happy sounds when he saw Jason. Their loving feelings were mutual.

He sat up in bed, holding and cuddling Christopher who soon fell asleep. We were alone with the baby, which was so nice. Sasumi had already been galvanised into air warden duty and was receiving her training over at Nu'uanu Park.

I put the baby in his cot and locked the bedroom door. I got into bed with my man, whose grin widened as I began to stroke his naked body.

"I'm so sorry they hurt you," I said.

He pulled me closer to him. It was a warm afternoon so he kicked off the bed clothes.

"I'm sorry you had to hear it. I know you were upset."

"Oh, darling, you were worried about me?"

"I love you, Tinder."

"I love you, too. Jason... I want to kill those Japanese officers."

He touched my face. "I dream of it. I hear that poor sailor screaming. I hear myself screaming. You're so gentle and loving... Tinder, you have to fuck me. I want to forget what happened."

We made long, slow love, my mouth never leaving his until his leaking cock kept slipping in my hand.

"Please, suck it," Jason moaned. He made a lot of noise as I sucked his sweet dick. I think he was sick of loving in silence. I reached under his body and grabbed his ass cheeks, shoving his cock deeper into my mouth.

"Arrrggh!" he shouted. Maybe Christopher thought it was music because the baby was sleeping right through our torrid lunchtime fuck.

I gently pulled my lover's legs apart.

"Don't be gentle, take me," he begged. "I need you, Tinder."

I didn't listen. I loved making love to him gently. I sucked his balls and his ass, taking my time building up the pressure in his body. He opened his legs wider and I knew he was really enjoying himself. He rocked back and forth on the bed, his sweet ass dancing against my tongue. I let him dictate the rhythm. This was his fuck, his joy. I wanted it to be simply exquisite for him.

When he moved again so that my tongue hit his ball sac, his legs began to shake. I knew he was going to come and moved up quickly to swallow as much as I could. He held my head, his eyes closed, his body jack-knifing off the bed.

"Tinder, Tinder, Tinder..." He kept up the mantra and I moved back to licking him again. As soon as he was ready, I tongued his cock head again. It twitched at my touch and I kissed the tip before opening my mouth to immediately take him in.

"Put it in me," he begged. "Put it in!"

Again I ignored him. I sucked his ass before slipping in a finger, taking it out, replacing it with my tongue.

"Stick it in! Now!"

I let my cock rub against his crack. Jason's face changed from desire to feral heat.

He reached around his own thigh and grabbed my cock.

"Now! Baby!"

I stuck it into him, worrying that I was hurting him. He gazed up at me.

"Fuck me, Tinder...I need you so much!"

I fucked him. I took it nice and slow, increasing my pace when he reached around, grabbing my ass and slapping me.

"Make me come! Fuck me harder!"

I took off in long, slow strokes, my lover's head tossing and turning on the pillow. A huge smile spread over his beautiful face. I knew this was it. I kept up the same pace as Jason looked deep into my eyes and came. I could feel his blessed relief melding our bodies together. I was stuck to him and him to me. I had never felt as close to anyone in my life.

He let out a cry that seemed to come from deep within his soul.

The world stopped. He wanted me to come too, and I did. I stayed inside him as my beautiful sweetheart lay, trembling against me, the aftershocks of his orgasms rocking his body.

And mine.

"Do that again," he said, smiling into my chest.

* * * *

Tuesday, February 17, 1942

We broke ground on the new property development on our street. Jason and I had worked hard on the plans and were pleased to provide so many locals with work. Kaonaka, our group leader in the fruit picking project, was our foreman.

It was a ritual in the islands that any new groundbreaking must include a small boy picking up the first handful of dirt and throwing it into the wheelbarrow. Little Christopher thought running his little fingers through the dirt then putting them in his mouth was great fun.

It wasn't a handful of dirt but we still thought it would bring us good luck. Everyone cheered and Christopher laughed. Sasumi took him back home to clean him up. As excited as we became, we were soon devastated when our digging turned up the body of a young blonde woman buried on a remote section of land that had only just been released to us by the government for military housing.

None of us knew how to react. It was awful. A few of the men sobbed and I was a wreck. She had been there for several weeks and was therefore in terrible condition, but I was pretty certain it was the woman I'd known as Melody Hampton.

Jason and I had a tough day, because we'd always hoped that Melody had some good reason other than death for leaving her baby son. I know what it's like to lose your mother. At least I'd got to know mine.

We called the police, starting with a friend of Jason's in the civil division. Of course, he arrived with a military counterpart. Since she was already dead, the cops acted like it was no big deal. The island's medical resources were swamped with the living and those on the brink of death.

The police, both civil and military, declined to pursue an investigation since her identification, found in her pocket, indicated it was Melody. Since she was a known prostitute, they had no desire to ruffle military feathers. Nobody knew who her family was. In life, she was used up and spat out. In death, she was an inconvenience.

Jason and I asked for her personal effects, such as her watch and ID card, to be given to us. I could hardly believe what had happened to Melody. It was a true tragedy. We decided we would hold a small funeral for her — very small — at the Chinese Cemetery at Manoa. Jason was able to procure a spot for her in the old children's section. I think she would have liked to be with them. The cemetery is well kept and we will make sure Christopher knows she is there. We will take him to visit her often.

This was not the first time a military figure had been associated with a violent crime against a woman in the islands. They were all hushed up. These types of attack were the reasons prostitutes were brought to Hotel Street in the first place. There were a few reports of rape, too, but since they involved Hawaiian women, little was done about them.

These were isolated incidents but they were there. And for us, they hurt, because a little boy was now without his mother.

* * * *

Friday, February 20, 1942

We suspended construction work until Monday since Dad and I were insistent that a *kahuna* bless the property before building resumed.

Our foreman, Sam, who wheedled the whole truth out of us, agreed. The *kahuna* was coming tomorrow, but today… Today we said goodbye to Melody.

Dad, Linda, Sasumi, Sam, Jason, Christopher and I gathered at the Manoa Cemetery to celebrate her life. It was a beautiful experience because the Chinese mourners wear red, which is a cheerful colour, I think. The deceased doesn't wear red, though, because the superstition is that red would turn the dead person into a ghost.

Melody was buried in a long white dress and shoes, both provided by Linda, who did us proud taking care of our girl.

We, the living, brought cakes and candies. Chinese mourners burn paper money to send their dead into the 'land beyond the lanterns' with food and cash. It felt festive and celebratory. Although she wasn't Chinese, Melody was family and the Buddhist priest who conducted the service sensed our profound grief.

I hadn't seen Melody's remains since she'd been transferred to the funeral home but she had been dusted with talcum powder and she was fully clothed, as tradition dictated. Her face had been covered in a yellow cloth.

Linda said a beautiful Christian prayer and then the skies opened up with rain.

"Ah," Sam Kanaka said, looking up at the sky, "she has walked the rainbow."

I hugged Sam, who hugged me back. His brother was a civilian cop and now that Sam knew everything he was determined to help our family get full custody of the baby. The old Hawaiian system of *hanai* adoption was still unspoken in white society but took place informally in the islands. Sam had three *hanai* children and promised to work hard to help us.

* * * *

Saturday, February 21, 1942

The *kahuna* said there were no bad spirits on the land where we had chosen to build. Sam, Jason, Dad and I watched as the frail-looking old man walked right to the spot where we had found Melody.

"She was killed someplace else. She was buried twice. I feel a uniform." His eyes widened. "Such anger." He shook it off, then exhaled. "I do not feel her soul here."

He lit some long branches and danced around a bit.

"How sad. How sad." He leaned against one of our shovels, lit a cigarette and smoked it with shaking fingers. "You must protect her boy."

Jason and I looked at each other. We would. We absolutely would. No matter what.

* * * *

Monday, March 16, 1942

In exchange for our silence—my words, not the military government's—Christopher was baptised at Our Lady of Peace Cathedral on Bishop Street. Jason and I chose this sacred church because Father Damien, the patron saint of the islands, had been ordained there. He loved and protected the lepers at the

Kalaupapa Colony on the island of Molokai. He was known to love all his flock—those who were sick or dying and the outcast.

And Melody had been an outcast.

Our little boy was accepted into the church as Christopher Jason McCartney and my father and Linda officially became his adoptive parents. Linda was the one who worked hard to secure the Cathedral for the baby's big day. Sam Kanaka became Christopher's godfather.

Christopher continued, however, to live with me and Jason, and my parents were able to see him as often as they wanted. Linda turned out to be a splendid grandma…though for a woman who made new clothes out of old ones professionally, I found it interesting that her great joy was buying him new ones.

Sasumi worked part-time in the house and part-time at the bank. She turned out to be the world's bossiest air warden.

Jason said he felt sorry for her future husband. She had no problem blasting whistles at you if she saw a little light in your windows. She seemed especially hard on the Hagaki family. I thought she might be sweet on their son, Iniro. Why else would she have volunteered to help Linda patrol their neighbourhood then headed right over to the Hagaki family, making trouble? I thought I would have to have a talk with her about her approach to romance.

I worked out of the house as an architect and my world revolved around Jason, the baby, and work.

My father adored Christopher and often drove around the island with him. Dad had begun to believe the story that he was my imaginary sister's child. He got a kick out of telling people that he was both the child's grandfather and his father. I thought he enjoyed the attention such notoriety brought him.

Jason, too, liked taking the baby to the bank, but I wasn't sure Christopher was quite ready to grasp the fascinating world of money. I did know he liked to try to eat coins that came his way...

We forged a wonderful life together and Jason never stopped reminding me how lucky we were. I knew we were and I always counted my blessings. Sometimes, when I was alone, I wondered if my mother and Christopher's were in heaven watching over us all. I sometimes wondered, do they drink tea in heaven? My mother loved tea.

* * * *

Wednesday, June 17, 1942

Two interesting things happened this week.

The one bright spot was the new tally of eight hundred members of the Hawaii Defence Volunteers. We were to begin training under the guidance of Army officers on Saturday at Queen Kapiolani Park.

In other news, the sex workers of Hotel Street went on strike two days ago, marching up and down with placards. They are still at it. The police, both civil and military, are furious because sailors and soldiers were on shore leave and wanted to get laid. There has been a virtual blackout on coverage of the strike. The ladies want more money. They are unlikely to get it. Servicemen aren't rich. They want more freedoms including things like having their own bank accounts and the right to ride a street car. These are basic freedoms Provost Marshal Frank Steer is likely to approve. He is a good man, and a fair one. Jason, of course, contacted him, offering to help in the women's quest to open savings accounts.

The other thing that happened was that Jean O'Hara slipped back into town and promptly got into trouble with the police. After another severe beating, she sued Chief Gabrielson for one hundred thousand dollars when he charged *her* with a crime. Though the police finally dropped their charges against her, she couldn't stay out of trouble. She booked rooms at the fancy Manoa Hotel with a couple of friends and began tricking out of them. They made so much noise dancing and screwing, somebody reported them to the police.

Though Jean's buddies managed to escape, she did not. When the cops busted into the room they found her lying on her bed reading a book. They didn't buy her act one bit.

She was arrested and charged and now faced jail time since civil courts had been disbanded and provost courts had no leniency when it came to civilians playing up.

* * * *

Friday, June 26, 1942

Like a lot of locals, I was fascinated by the pending Jean O'Hara trial. I grabbed one of the last few seats in the courtroom. Sasumi was desperate to attend so she came with me. Jason took the baby to work with him.

I was shocked at how tough the provost court was on Jean. They knew the cops had regularly beaten her up but this seemed of little importance to the court. The participants seemed bent on destroying her. It was surprising. I mean, she was, after all, not the only one having fun in that swanky hotel room.

Jean caught my eye at one point and winked.

"Do you know her?" Sasumi asked.

"Yes, I do."

"I have read her book," she whispered, giggling behind her hand.

I was impressed with how pretty and demure Jean looked. I almost laughed, actually. She was wearing one of Linda's newly remodelled fashions. She single-handedly turned Linda into one of the most sought-after seamstresses in the islands.

When the court sentenced Jean to six months in jail, everybody was aghast…except for Jean.

She looked quite happy, actually. She smiled at the judge and said, "Thank you, Your Honour. I plan to take a nice, long rest."

What a woman!

Epilogue

Four Years Later…
Friday, August 9, 1946

For the people of Hawaii, the war is *finally* and officially over today. With the homecoming of the 442nd Division aboard the Army troop transport, the *Waterbury-Victory* in Honolulu Harbor, all our sons, brothers, husbands, lovers and friends are home and the Hawaiian Islands can return to the life for which they are known.

The harbour was packed with well-wishers. I held Christopher in my arms and laughed when he kept screaming, "*Aloha!*"

The arriving soldiers all screamed back the word echoing around the island.

Aloha.

Though the fifteenth of August, 1945, was the day Japan surrendered, for the islands the war was not over until every last serviceman was home.

And now, it is.

Our island home can once again be a place of refuge and relaxation, welcoming all who need her comfort and her grace.

Sasumi married Iniro, the son of my father's neighbour, Mr Hagaki, and they are very happy. She is Jason's most trusted employee, though she only works three days a week since she and Iniro have one son and are expecting another baby any day now.

My father still has a huge crush on her.

Dad is still married to Linda, who has a thriving business as a seamstress on King Street. Jason is her biggest investor.

Christopher McCartney is five years old and a handsome, happy child. He is learning hula from me, swimming from Jason, and poker from my father. He goes to kindergarten at Kaiulani School and his favourite place to play is around and on the banyan tree in the courtyard, which started as a cutting from the Princess's Ainahau estate.

I feel I have passed my mother's love for Ainahau on to him. I take him to the estate almost every day. I want him to know it, to love it, to feel it in his bones before it's all gone.

He loves to read and play, but he loves music, singing, and finger painting the most. One day, Jason and I will explain to him about his mother and that she loved him very, very much. We have kept her suitcase containing what little we have of her belongings so that he has some…touchstone—a keepsake of her memory. It is his to do with as he pleases.

The last few years have brought many blessings and, as the Chinese people like to say, 'interesting times'. President Roosevelt came to visit for three days in July of 1944. He asked to visit the amputee wards at the

Saint Louis Provisional Hospital. He was taken around in his wheelchair, something he never let the public see. I heard on the radio that he was near tears by the time he left those wards. He stayed as a guest at Queen's Surf, which by then had been transformed into a place of rest for the military. It is now once again a very busy, successful restaurant.

Jean O'Hara was the only prostitute to serve time in Oahu State Prison for her 'crimes'. She scandalised and titillated the islands by publishing her manifesto, *Honolulu Harlot*. Upon her release from jail in 1943, she was last seen driving off with her new husband in a brand new vehicle. She vanished from public life and was never heard from again. I heard a rumour her husband had smuggled her to one of the outer islands and that she probably ended her days in quiet luxury. I like to think so. But what do I know? And I am not one to gossip.

I never heard about any of the other prostitutes after the brothels were all shut down by government order on the twenty-first of September, 1944. Most of the women were shipped back to the mainland immediately. A few managed to stay and work in unregulated brothels with pimps who controlled them and charged up to a hundred dollars a trick, which most servicemen couldn't pay.

Now, they are all gone.

The Hotel Street of today is embarrassed about its cheap brothels, but I see no shame in what these women did for our fighting men. For many young sailors and soldiers, these women gave comfort—and yes, they gave sex—to many, many men who lived...and just as many who died in combat. For some men, this was their first sexual encounter with a woman, and, in some tragic cases, their *only* sexual experience before being killed in battle.

The Hawaii Defence Volunteers disbanded long before the war ended last year. There were many reasons for this, but volunteer corps just lost interest when it became evident that we all needed to think ahead. The Japanese threat was gone long before they officially surrendered.

I think we were all just sick of living in fear.

Jason and I bought about forty pieces of land and we've built homes for dozens of families. We like to say that we were there for the start of many new lives. We now share a magnificent, picturesque piece of land in Turtle Bay on the North Shore with my father and Linda. We will build two houses on it. The best, most beautiful houses I can design.

I still work from home and Christopher has shown great interest in my drafting tools. However, his fondness is for sticking my pencils up his nose, not drawing with them...yet. He continues to have four people contributing to his daily life who love him. As we say in the islands, it takes *ohana* – a family – to raise a kid.

Jason and I are still madly in love. I hope we always will be.

He has occasional nightmares but seems much better now that most of those who'd been on board the SS *Malama* have been released from their torments. The crew members were held at Woo Sung for most of the war, then transferred to Hokkaido. Most have admitted they were tortured. So far, we know of only one death.

Jason is still the most handsome, most wonderful man I have ever met, and the kindest, too. I love him more than I can say. He has my whole heart and I know, for me, there will never be another.

As for the people of Hawaii—those who should wish to attempt to attack us and invade us again should know that we are a peaceful people. We are all about love. Our islands have always welcomed strangers as friends we have not yet met. For those who wish us harm, I can only say, *Aloha* to you…

AVENGING
HEART

Author's Note

The bank depicted in this story is fictional but Chinese-owned banks were among the first to do business in Honolulu. I have based Jason's story in part on oral histories of Oahu's first Chinese residents. Though fictional, his experiences are similar to those of the hard-working men and women who lived in the Hawaiian Islands before and immediately after World War II.

My sincere thanks to all my readers for accompanying me on this fourth and final chapter in Jason and Tinder's love story.

I would especially like to thank my dear friend, my chosen brother, Gary Hill whose research efforts gave me the idea for this story. The events depicted such as the prison riot in Oahu on March 31, 1947 and United Air Lines' first commercial flight into the islands are historically accurate.

I'd also like to thank the wonderful team at Total-e-Bound—our awesome publisher, Claire Siemaszkiewicz, Nicki Richards, Heidi Blakey, and my patient and loving editor, Stacey Birkel.

Finally, to all the men, women and children who lived through, worked and sacrificed so much during World War II...the documentaries, home movies and flash footage I have watched of the VJ Day celebrations in Honolulu on August 14, 1945 do not do justice to your pain and horror. To quote filmmaker Richard Sullivan, 'none of us would be here without you'.

— A.J. Llewellyn

Chapter One

Monday, April 21, 1947
Honolulu, Hawaii

My life in Honolulu, like so many others in the islands, remains restricted under the dark cloud of World War II, even though the war has been over for almost two years. Every day we hear of ordinary families struggling to regain their homes and plantations that had been taken over by the military during the war. Though Martial Law was abolished in 1944, the US Supreme Court has just today, finally, declared it unconstitutional.

Just as we began to think we could put the past behind us, my partner Jason and I learned on the radio this morning that the people of the isolated, outer island of Ni'ihau are still being subjected to the most austere restrictions of all.

Thanks to the island's feudal ownership by the Robinson family, the residents of Ni'ihau have no access to news, cannot own radios, and do not have adequate educational facilities or medical care.

Imagine. A life with no news and no music? I became instantly despondent. Jason immediately began plotting how to get radios, first aid kits, books, toys and newspapers over to the island. The words *'They live in complete subservience to the island's paternal owners'* reverberated in my brain, rendering me immobile.

"This is terrible," Jason said, getting out of our bed and picking up his ever-present to-do list. I am a worrier — Jason is a doer. A born doer, all the way.

My name is Tinder McCartney, and Jason and I have been together for six years. It is my privilege to love him and care for him, and our precious son Christopher, who is a robust, healthy, happy little boy of five. We inherited him in 1942 when he was just two weeks old. His mother Melody had been a prostitute at the same hotel I worked at — only fate handed me Jason, and Melody... Well, poor Melody got knocked up by a US military officer. She'd lived in fear of him and paid dearly for her relationship with him.

He murdered her.

So, now, Christopher is ours. I have a dim memory of his father who came to see us once. I never forget a face and I could identify him if I ever saw him again, but now Christopher is safe and loved.

"Daddy?" He knocked on our door. I glanced at my husband. We might not be legally married men, but we are husbands. In every way. Jason looked up at me from his position on the floor. We were both naked and I'd hoped for some early morning fun until Ni'ihau's problem became our challenge. We both laughed.

"No rest for the wicked," my handsome man said. We rushed around getting dressed and opened the door to our little boy. He barrelled in, dressed only in pyjama bottoms since the weather was so humid. He is such a beautiful child. He loves us both equally but Jason was closest. Christopher put his arms up to Jason, who snatched him up, hoisted him into the air and kissed him.

Christopher laughed. Then it was my turn. I love to see him with Jason, who could not love a child more. Everything we do is for our son. He looks nothing like Jason, who is Chinese, but he is blond, like me. We put out the rumour that he is my dead sister's child when we first took him in. He was the child nobody wanted but now he has four adults who fiercely love him, the other two being my father and step-mother. Dad and Linda adore our rambunctious little handful. They have been the perfect cover for us since I don't really have a dead sister. I was an only child, but even my dad has come to believe the story. He and Linda are Christopher's legal parents, but he is *our* child.

"Tinder," he said, showing me his treasure. We had been careful to teach him to call me by my given name since I was technically, in the eyes of the world, his uncle. Jason was Daddy. I checked on Christopher's trophy. It was a gecko, though the poor little guy looked the worse for wear in my son's trusty grip. He adores animals but has to learn not to squeeze them to death out of love.

It took Jason and me a few minutes to coax Christopher into releasing the gecko to our bedroom windowsill. He cried hot tears when the little yellow lizard ran to safety.

"We'll get you a dog," I promised.

"When?" he asked me, more tears pooling in his big, beautiful, blue eyes. I felt a tug at my heart. My mother would have loved him. I missed her so much but she died before Pearl Harbor was bombed. I am glad she didn't have to suffer, though I miss her smile, her laughter and her wonderful hugs.

"Soon," I promised.

"Bacon," Christopher said. All three of us laughed. Next to getting a dog, Christopher's other obsession in life is food. He's in good company. We both love to eat and Jason is a generous husband who frequently takes us out to dinner. One of the most prominent bankers in Honolulu, he also owns several small businesses and his shipping line brings in luxuries from Japan and China so that the people of Honolulu can have things like rice and silk stockings. These were hard to come by during the war. We also have an icebox filled with ice cream, just because we can.

Sometimes I wake up and think we are still in the war. There are sirens and then we are placed under curfew. It all seems designed to keep us afraid…keep us in line. Sometimes I think Honolulu is just one great big Ni'ihau.

I carried our son into the kitchen. Gripping my hips with his strong legs, he reached over to the radio on the countertop and turned it on. The Andrews Sisters' jaunty song *Rum and Coca Cola* was playing. An ardent music lover as much as we were, Christopher began singing the lyrics at the top of his voice, making me laugh. I wasn't sure a five-year-old should sing about drinking rum, but he had no idea what the song was about. He just loved to sing. He shrugged himself out of my arms and began dancing around the kitchen.

A shadow crossed the windowpane. I glanced outside. Was somebody out there? I checked in both directions as far as I could see but nobody was there.

"Tinder, what's wrong?" Jason asked, coming right to my side. He kept a protective arm around my waist.

"I think there's somebody out there."

Without a word, Jason took the gun from the top shelf of the cabinet beside me. I hated that thing but he felt we needed it. It wasn't paranoia. Christopher's mother had been murdered. We'd been the ones to discover her body and so we were aware, more than most, that life wasn't all tropical rain and sunshine.

He went outside. I waited. Jason came to the window and shook his head. "*Nothing*," he mouthed. I relaxed a little and began preparing breakfast. As I beat the eggs with cheese and fresh herbs, I looked out of the window to see him twirling Christopher in the air. Jason had shoved the gun into the waistband in back of his trousers, but I still didn't want that weapon anywhere near the baby. I rapped on the window and shook my head.

Jason caught my gaze and must have read my message because he soon returned, stowing the gun back in the cupboard behind the soup bowls. He wrestled with Christopher in the living room as I heated a couple of skillets for the bacon, eggs and slices of thick Portuguese bread. It was such a luxury not to have to scrape butter anymore.

"Bacon!" Christopher shrieked.

"Help me set the table," Jason told our son.

"Okay, Daddy!"

Christopher's idea of setting the table is to throw spoons and forks on top of it and laugh himself silly. He likes to make noise and he gets a kick out of the way he so easily entertains us.

My men were hungry. Christopher took turns sitting in his own chair, then both our laps, and as soon as we'd demolished breakfast, he turned his attention to his beach toys. He knew our routine and the early mornings were just for him and me and Waikiki Beach.

Jason took the dishes into the kitchen. He gave me what I have come to call the 'hooded look'. I knew he was anxious for the morning fuck he'd missed and, frankly, so was I. Leaving the dishes in the sink, I filled a bucket with water and gave Christopher some toys to play with on the living room floor. He'd be all right for a few minutes on his own. I closed and locked the kitchen door, though Jason always teased me about that.

"I'm going to help Daddy in the bathroom for just a little while," I told my small son, who was already fully engaged in submerging his favourite plastic toys in the bucket. He loved washing his rubber duckies and the shovel he used to make sandcastles at the beach. With any luck, I could coax him into helping me with household chores when he was older.

"Okey, dokey!" It was his mantra and I thanked my lucky stars to have a child obsessed with water. It could distract him for hours.

I gave him a kiss and reminded myself not to squeeze his little apple cheeks because he didn't like that much and, besides, everybody else did that. I ran to the bathroom and found Jason anxiously waiting for me. His cock was hard as he stepped out of his trousers.

Falling to my knees as I closed the door behind me, I leant forward and captured that perfect specimen with my lips. Jason pulled back so that his cock fell out of my mouth. He moved forwards and I sucked him in again. He played with me a few more times, teasing me. He knew it would drive me crazy if he ever actually took that beautiful cock away from me.

I sucked him all the way in and he let out a groan. From the first time we made love, I adored the beautiful monster that had become my privilege to tame. I had no idea why but the more time we spent together, the more intense our connection became. We sometimes didn't know what to say to our straight friends whose own romantic passions had waned. I couldn't get enough of Jason and I liked sending him off to work each morning with a big smile on his face.

Coming off his cock for a moment, I gazed up at him. "Turn around, Jason."

He grinned down at me, but finally complied. He turned and I grabbed his hips, licking along his ass crack. He pushed into my tongue, obviously liking what I was doing to him. He loved having his ass licked, sucked and the occasional finger inside him, but fucking him was out of the question. He'd tried it a couple of times but I think he enjoys fucking me too much to be the bottom again anytime soon. He let me have my fun until he just couldn't take it anymore. He turned and swivelled his hips until I caught his cock with my lips and tongue.

Jason held my head as I took him all the way in. His balls bushed against my chin. He was so close and sometimes he forgot that I needed to move my face. I tried to release his grip but he was too far gone.

"Tinder...Tinder...Tinder..." He moaned my name softly as he came. His cock hit the roof of my mouth, hot liquid splashing my throat. He slumped against the sink as I kept sucking and swallowing. I held his ass in both hands, wanting him closer, harder.

His body shook as I drew back with my mouth, allowing my tongue to tease his shaft, lightly licking the sensitive head.

"God, Tinder..."

He didn't need to say another word.

"I wanted to fuck you," he said, frowning.

"You will, when you come home for lunch." I kissed him quickly. The feverish haze to his eyes told me he was already thinking about it. Good. I liked keeping him hot and anxious for me.

He suddenly shook his head and laughed.

I let myself out of the bathroom and left him to bathe in peace. Christopher had spilt water everywhere and, when I walked in, he let loose with a laugh that only encouraged mine as well. Great parents we were. My father often accused us of egging him on and I'm ashamed to admit I'm guilty as charged. He is a good little boy, however, and water is easily dried.

After I'd cleaned the floors, we packed a tote bag with his favourite toys and a beach hat for me. Jason rushed into the living room to hug us as Christopher fought me over what he was going to wear. He only wanted to wear his swim trunks and not his shorts over them.

"You're only going to the beach," Jason said. "Take some clothes with you for later."

He was right. Coming home, Christopher knew we'd stop at the Waikiki Pharmacy for a milkshake at the soda fountain. He would allow me to dress him properly for that. He supervised as I packed a pair of shorts, underpants and a short-sleeved shirt into a second bag. I rushed to the bedroom I shared with Jason to change and got the spooky feeling somebody was outside again.

Once more, I checked. Nothing. I was getting paranoid.

No. I wasn't. Our front gate had just closed. By the time I rushed out of the front door, whoever it was had long gone.

Jason wasn't concerned when I told him.

"Fruit thieves," he said. This might have been true. We had a garden with all kinds of fruits and people had been known to filch them. Christopher allowed me to slide his feet into leather sandals. He was the most stylish little boy we knew, thanks to his doting grandparents and to Jason's Chinatown shipping contacts.

"Ready, Tinder." Christopher tucked his hand into mine. Jason hugged and kissed us both, picked up his briefcase, and we all walked outside. He drove off in his new Ford truck as I distracted Christopher by showing him a huge spider web on our garden. There is nothing deadly in paradise. Even the spiders are friendly. We had a host of yellow happy-face spiders that got busy every night. Christopher loved the smiling faces nature had painted on their backs and he knew all three spiders who'd lived in our yard for over a year.

"Mickey!" he shouted. Almost all of the critters who came our way were named Mickey since Mickey Mouse was his favourite character in the whole wide world. His passion in life was to see Mickey's short films at the Waikiki Theater at the Saturday matinees with my father.

He laughed as the spider zigzagged along its web. As soon as Jason had gone, we crossed the road. Our family home on Kuhio Avenue was just a block from the beach. Gone were the endless reams of barbed wire that had punctuated the sand before Pearl Harbor had even been attacked. We saw lots of people on the beach, the women in various bikinis that had suddenly become all the rage.

Christopher broke free from me and charged towards the water. I deposited our belongings on the sand and kicked off my shoes, pants and shirt and ran into the freezing shallows behind him.

We usually rented a surfboard on the beach for a dime, but Waikiki Willie wasn't around that morning. Christopher didn't mind. He wanted to build a sandcastle right near the water's edge. His work was so intricate and his focus so complete that I convinced myself he was taking after me and would one day become an architect too.

As we turned to fetch a few of his toys to guard his moat, I noticed a man in a dark suit watching us from the palm garden of the Moana Hotel. As soon as he caught my gaze, he stepped back into the lush foliage, but I was certain he'd been staring at us. The thought dimmed my pleasure in the simple joy of taking Christopher to the beach.

The waves crashed my son's castle to an unrecognisable blob.

"Oh, no!" He chortled, gazing up at me.

I glanced back at the man who'd been standing there, but he was gone.

"One more swim, angel?"

"Okey, dokey."

We ran back to the surf—Christopher a fearless and natural swimmer with a strong stroke. He pointed out to the horizon.

"Ship!"

"That's right." I kissed his wet head and he leapt into my arms. We dodged a couple of waves together and he pointed to the ship again.

"*Matson!*"

I almost fell over, I laughed so hard. He knew every cruise and cargo ship thanks to Jason's work and loved *Lei* Day—the day the cruise ships came into Honolulu Harbor—so much that we planned to take him on a sea voyage with my parents. We just couldn't decide where we wanted to go.

Jason wanted to go to China and Hong Kong. I wanted to go to New York. My parents felt we should go to San Francisco and look up Melody's family but they had never shown any interest in the baby the few times we'd contacted them and I didn't want Christopher to have any memories of being rejected.

Thanks to us, he was alive. We'd saved him from a well-meaning shopkeeper who had taken him in as a favour to Melody, only she had no idea how to look after a baby. As a gay couple, neither did we, but we sure learned fast.

We took a few more waves together, Christopher jumping around in my arms, and then I saw the man again. He had a camera!

This was too much. I waded back to shore with Christopher and dried him off. We walked along the beach hand in hand—I, as usual, bogged down with carrying everything. Christopher sang songs and pointed out birds and flowers to me. The man watched us walk by. As soon as we reached the beach taps near the hotel garden, Christopher stood under the cold shower spray, letting me rinse him off. I dried him quickly and dressed him, grooming his hair with my fingers since I'd forgotten his comb.

I glanced over my shoulder but the man was gone. I was getting paranoid. I had to ask myself, *Why would anyone be watching us?*

My heart almost stopped.

Before Pearl Harbor had been attacked, I'd worked very briefly as a male prostitute on Hotel Street. Sometimes I caught the gazes of servicemen I'd, er…dated…but I didn't think I'd ever seen this man before. He frightened me. I had no idea why he was watching us, but I didn't like it. At all.

We crossed the road and made our way to the pharmacy. The soda jerk greeted us like family...and we were family. We'd been going there since Christopher was a baby.

"Do you want a milkshake, angel?" I asked as I hoisted him onto one of the fountain stools.

Christopher nodded eagerly. He was a chocolate man, like my father. He watched intently as his drink was prepared, grinning up at me. There was so much love and trust in his little face. I adored him.

Tears pricked at the back of my eyes but I had no idea why.

No...I knew. The three of us were happy together and Jason and I never stopped counting our blessings. I helped Christopher drink his frothy milkshake. I kept checking the doorway for the man in the dark suit but he didn't show up and I began to breathe easier. Christopher drained his glass then wanted to check out the pharmacy's shelves. He always liked to keep abreast of the latest toys in stock. Mind you, he wasn't lacking for those. We paid for our drink and wandered over to the children's section. He skidded past the baby bottles and infant formula to a brand new display of steel toy trucks and cars.

"Tinder!" he shrieked, eyes agog. His hand fell on a fire chief's car. He picked it up, holding it to his chest.

"Do you want the coal truck, too?" I asked.

He stared at it, but picked up the grocery truck with the little yellow ladder instead. The vehicles were ninety-eight cents apiece. There were four in the display, including a school bus. He would be starting school in September so this would be fun, I decided. I picked up the remaining two vehicles as he ran the fire chief's car along the polished floor. I paid for the toys at the counter. We had a bit of a fight over which car he'd hold on to as we walked home. Once again, he watched as I put his toys away and he gave me his hand.

"Tinder," the cashier whispered, "that man is staring at you."

I glanced up but he was gone. Now I knew I wasn't imagining things and I was anxious to get home.

Christopher was so excited with his new belongings he couldn't wait to play with them when we arrived. He grabbed some dirt from our garden for the coal truck and played as I picked vegetables for lunch and dinner. We had a magnificent garden in the backyard, but as soon as I'd gathered enough for both meals, I made him come inside. I had a bad feeling about the man who'd been watching us.

As I prepared our food, I kept an ear out for Jason. I didn't want to call him and worry him but as soon as walked in the door he said, "There was a man across the road watching the house."

"Is he wearing a dark suit?"

He frowned. "Yes."

I told him about the beach and the pharmacy. "What do you think he wants?"

"No idea, but I'm not going back to work. I chased him off just now but I don't like the idea of leaving you two alone with some...marauder following you." He paused. "As a matter of fact, I'm going to call the police."

I felt a lot better knowing that Jason was going to stay home and that the police would now be involved. I had just finished making our lunch of fish with coconut vegetables and rice when our local constable arrived.

Christopher knew him well and ran to greet him, showing him his new grocery truck. Officer Hsu picked our son up in his arms.

"My God," I said, looking out of the window. "That man. He's out there again!"

Officer Hsu put my son into my arms and dashed out of the door. Jason wanted the gun but I wouldn't let him take it. He rushed out after the policeman and they were gone so long I started to worry. And watched.

And waited. And waited some more.

Finally Jason and Officer Hsu returned.

"I have his licence number but he got away," Officer Hsu said. "You are to call me if you see that man anywhere near your house again. Do you understand?"

"Yes, of course," I said.

"Understood," Jason said.

Christopher sensed our tension and lapsed into silence. He wasn't used to any unpleasantness and didn't seem to know how to react. I kissed his sweet little head and held him tighter.

"Play with me, Tinder."

"Lunch first," I insisted, inviting the policeman to join us.

"It smells so good I can't say no." He beamed at me. Christopher had a good time, but three adults around him kept checking out of the windows for the man in the dark suit.

That evening, we abandoned our dinner plans and went over to visit my father and Linda at their wonderful home in Turtle Bay on the North Shore. We loved the other side of the island. There were no traffic lights and miles and miles of sugar cane farms. Dole pineapple cannery had acres of farm, too. But it was a beach community. A country beach family. People often rode horses and buggies and stopped by the homes out there offering to sell fresh eggs, churned butter and taro roots.

The main road along the shore hugged the rugged coast. Much of it was still hard-packed dirt. Some of it had been paved, but chickens and turkeys roamed it in varying degrees of speed.

Quite often they wound up as food.

To me, Turtle Bay was a reminder of my childhood in the islands. The tempo was slow and time seemed to stand still. The air always carried the mingled scent of salt air and kerosene lamps. It was the smell I was raised with and it still had a hold on my soul.

When we arrived, Dad and Linda greeted us with great excitement. Inside the house, Linda fussed over us with tea and warm cakes from the oven. They became concerned when we told them what had happened, but they made us feel a lot better by taking care of us and insisting we stay the night. Jason and I felt secure in the knowledge that Christopher was safe in their remote mountaintop home.

Linda bathed him and read to him. In the living room Dad wanted more details about what had happened back at our house.

"I think it's a case of mistaken identity," he said when he'd heard everything. "Or it's somebody who wants your house."

Yes, that could have been it. We'd been busy building and designing homes even during the war. Our house was beautiful, but it was also our home. It wasn't for sale.

"I think you should all come back here for a few days," Dad said. "This is your home too, you know. You built it for us." He smiled. Dad was so happy these days with his wife and the little business they'd forged out of her sewing. Linda was one of the busiest dressmakers on the island. She made custom orders that Dad delivered by car for her. He also collected bolts of fabric and other necessities for the garments she made for the Chinatown stores.

Dad warmed to his theme. "Jason can just as easily drive to work from here and you, Tinder, can work here. Just bring whatever plans you're working on and don't forget we have plenty of clothes for Christopher."

The truth was, I didn't have any major work lined up. I had a few tentative irons in the fire, but we both liked the idea of staying with our family for a few days. Jason would need a couple of suits but Dad said he could borrow his.

That night, Jason and I slept in the guest bedroom with Christopher between us, Jason's arm around us both. Christopher had his own room but neither of us felt comfortable being away from him, so after Linda tucked our little boy into bed, Jason carried him into our room. We whisper-talked as our child slept and convinced each other that the man in the dark suit was a mistake...or something innocent. But I had a bad feeling.

And it kept me awake all night.

* * * *

Tuesday, April 22, 1947

Dad and Linda did their best to keep our minds off the worrisome stranger and succeeded very well. After a hearty breakfast, they took us over to the nearby sugar train and we went for several rides on it. Christopher thought it was the best thing since Mickey

Mouse and especially loved the long sugar cane stalk the train driver gave him after his final voyage. He sucked on it as we drove back into Honolulu later that day. We planned to pack a few things and go back to Turtle Bay that evening.

As usual, I sat in the back seat next to Christopher, who could be unruly in the car. The three of us had so much fun together that I almost convinced myself the man in the dark suit was nothing to worry about.

And then we arrived home.

Officer Hsu was parked outside. His expression grim, he came into the house with us. I made coffee and, with Christopher distracted by his cars and trucks, Officer Hsu said in a low voice, "The man following you is a private investigator."

Jason and I were shocked.

"What does he want with us?" Jason asked.

"I don't know. He's a local guy, bit of a beach weasel if you ask me. His name is Sooty Maxwell. Weird name, I know, but he got it because he's been known to even hide in people's chimneys to get information on them."

"Are you serious?" Jason looked worried.

"As a heart attack." Officer Hsu glanced at our son who was busy with his toys.

"Rumour has it on the vine that Sooty just got a job with a bit of money behind him. He's been asking *a lot* of questions about the two of you."

"About us? Why?" I asked.

Officer Hsu took the coffee I handed him. "You are both very well liked in these islands, Tinder. Nobody's told Sooty a blessed thing. He asked about Christopher and he knows he's your sister's child, but he seems to have other ideas... Now, none of this is any of my business, but if you ever need to talk, I hope you know you have a friend in me."

We were going to need his friendship sooner than either of us thought. There was a knock at the front door and Jason took charge, accepting delivery of a telegram.

It was addressed to me and it had come from San Francisco. I read it, and re-read it and couldn't quite believe it. I handed it to my lover, who stared at it.

"Melody's parents are coming here?" His disbelief matched my own. "They arrive...by...plane on Saturday and they say they want..."

His voice broke. "Christopher."

Chapter Two

Officer Hsu had befriended us after the war was over. He was one of the many people who'd been displaced during the military's takeover of many parts of the island. He'd been just out of high school and had wanted to be a police officer, but had volunteered for military duty. His family home had been forcibly evacuated whilst he'd been shipped out to the war in the Pacific.

His people, the loveliest Korean-American family we knew, had only been allowed to move back in six months after VJ Day on August 14, 1945, and that was only because his father had walked into Jason's office begging for help. If it hadn't been for Jason, a lot of Asian families would have been displaced for many more months.

We'd suffered, too. I had volunteered Jason's house to the military whilst he'd been at sea on a clandestine mission for the government. It took us even longer to get the house back, but Officer Hsu, first name Oliver, was, ironically, our immediate neighbour. We cleaned our house, which had been treated disgracefully by the military family stationed there. We repainted, restored the koa wood floors to their lustrous shine, and Christopher and I planted new flowers in the garden. At Oliver's request, we rented our house to his sister and her family and befriended them all.

Oliver, being the father of a four-year-old boy, had taken a shine to us and little Kimo often played with Christopher.

"What's going on?" Oliver asked now. I glanced at Jason. How far did we go in spilling our secrets? Jason was staring at the telegram. It was as if he was willing the words to change, but they were committed to my memory where they unfortunately would live forever. Those hateful, horrid words.

We want our grandson. We want to bring Christopher home. Stop.

No, never. They couldn't have him. Over my dead body. By the look on Jason's face, it would be over his dead body, too. *Stop.*

"Christopher isn't Tinder's sister's son," Jason said. His voice was still hoarse. I handed him a cup of coffee and he gulped at it.

"I figured as much. Who is his mother?" Oliver glanced from Jason to me and back again. In his on-duty hours he was Officer Hsu. In his civilian hours he was Oliver. I had no idea which one we were talking to right now and I was petrified to find out.

"During the war, a woman I knew in Chinatown — actually, both of us knew her — came to us and told us she was looking after a white woman's baby." Jason paused, sipping his coffee. I felt a flood of relief that he wasn't about to mention my salacious past.

"The baby was Christopher and his mother's name was Melody. She had worked for a short time as a prostitute on Hotel Street but had left the islands when she'd become pregnant. We hadn't even known she was back. She'd returned and, from all accounts, she'd been working again but she left the baby with the woman in Chinatown."

"Who was this woman?"

Jason looked Oliver right in the eye and lied. "She died a couple of years ago, but she was a shopkeeper." The truth was that we had helped her move to Hong Kong where her son had begun a shipping business, working with Jason. She had kept our secret and she had no judgements on my past. We'd been happy to help her.

My lover shrugged. "She was a nice lady but elderly and she couldn't care for the baby. He was very sick and she didn't have the means to help him. She asked us to step in, and we did. We took him home with us."

"We saved his life," I interjected. "He had a milk fever."

Jason was nodding. "I had to bribe a Chinatown doctor to get us infant formula for him. It was touch and go there for a while. We lived in Chinatown at the time and took care of the baby around the clock. We grew to love him and he stayed with us."

Jason turned his head to watch our son for a moment.

"We kept him, wondering if we'd ever see Melody again. We didn't. Tinder's father and step-mother adopted him legally when Melody was found dead."

"Dead?" Oliver asked. He looked so agog with this story that he hadn't touched a drop of coffee.

"Like I said, she was a prostitute and she'd been murdered. When we began construction work on the land behind the house here, the work crew dug up her body. I can't tell you how devastated we all were."

"Did you report this to the police?"

"Of course we did. Nobody cared about her. Only us." Jason looked older all of a sudden. Every word he said was true. "We held a funeral for her and she's buried at the Chinese Cemetery at Manoa. We wanted to keep her close, and one day our son will know everything."

There was a significant pause. Jason and I watched our tow-headed boy but he was completely absorbed with his toys.

"How did you know her?" Hsu asked, looking directly at me.

We'd rehearsed this discussion between us many times and it had been our official story in the first letter we'd sent Melody's family in San Francisco.

"She was roommates at one time with Jean O'Hara."

I let the name of Hotel Street's most notorious and long-since-vanished prostitute sink into Hsu's brain.

"Jean O'Hara?" He stared at me.

"Jason and I actually bought a house from her. She was worried about Melody because she was living with Jean and was supposed to be working with Jean in her house." I glanced at Jason. I hated giving up Melody's secrets like this, but the train had left the station and I couldn't stop it.

My lover nodded and I continued.

"From what Jean told us, Melody and a third girl rented rooms in the house, but Melody was flighty…and, Jean learned, Melody had come back to Honolulu with a baby. Jean never saw the baby. Melody kept him in Chinatown and paid the woman there to care for him. She must have loved Christopher a lot because she went every day to breastfeed him. And then one day she just didn't come back."

We were all silent for a moment.

Jason picked up the story. "I don't think Jean was happy with Melody because she was dating a military man and Jean suspected he was the baby's father." He smiled all of a sudden. "She wasn't a soft girl, Jean—she didn't believe in romance and took a dim view of working girls falling for their tricks."

"Oh, my God." Hsu sloshed coffee onto the floor. I took the cup from him and mopped up the hot liquid with a clean cloth. He had turned bright red, clearly embarrassed and yet...fascinated by our story.

"Sorry," Jason said.

"Tinder." Christopher toddled over to me and I picked him up. I walked away with him in my arms, listening to the conversation as I pulled out some of his other toys from the chest beside the sofa.

"Jean talked a tough game," Jason said, "but she was a good woman underneath all the bravado. I guess she gave our names to the woman in Chinatown as likely candidates to help her...and the baby."

Hsu stared at Jason. The facts we'd given him were all true, but we'd left out a few salient points that were really none of his business.

"But why *you*?"

"We all knew each other in Chinatown."

"She and I had the same doctor," I said. "I ran into her there one day and she told me she was pregnant. She wanted to keep her baby and so she returned to the mainland."

"And if you know anything about Tinder and me, we helped everybody during the war," Jason said. "I like to think we still do."

Hsu pointed at me. "I know you chartered a fishing boat to go and rescue Jason."

"Sure I did."

"You two are something else…wow. This is quite a story. And you know Jean O'Hara, too!"

"Correction." Jason held up a hand. "We *knew* her. Once we'd paid her for the house she split town. Nobody's seen her since the brothels were shut down."

"She sounds like a very selfish woman," Hsu said. "Did she report this Melody woman as missing?"

Jason and I glared at him. It was a harsh condemnation of Jean, who'd been regularly beaten and robbed and even incarcerated for her crime of prostitution by the police—the very men who had regulated the vice in Chinatown.

"She did her best, considering her infamy. You should also know she'd just sustained a severe beating by the police," Jason said.

Oliver recoiled. "Really?" He scrunched up his nose.

"They raided the house. The girls were all beaten up. Jean took the brunt of the cops' aggression. That savage attack destroyed her teeth. They knocked out a couple and she had bridgework that needed to be fixed. She couldn't see out of one eye. We came to look at the house and buy it but she was in agony." Jason glanced at me. "You will find this made up the bulk of her trial and still she was convicted."

I nodded. "She wasn't looking for sympathy." I hadn't thought about this for a long time and the ugly incident flooded back to my mind. "We took her to the dentist and then we brought her home. She was taking opium drops for the pain but she still wanted to do business. She was a tough cookie. We paid her the money for the house and that was the last we saw of her."

"I think she cared about Melody, though." Jason picked up Christopher, who'd charged over to him, anxious for attention, his little arms outstretched. "She'd sent her to one of the other islands, but for some reason, Melody came back. Again. She must have been really in love with the man she'd been with.

"From what Jean told us she tried to warn Melody she was playing with fire. She said working girls never married officers." He sighed. "But they don't usually get killed by them, either."

"Do you know who he is?" Hsu asked.

"Not by name. We saw him once." Jason frowned at the memory. "He came to our old place in Chinatown in the back of a car. He wound down his window." Oh, I remembered that day well. The man had been horrible. "He warned us not to go after the baby's father. We never did." Jason looked at me, misery etched on his handsome features.

"We also had a visit from two officers in the military police department. As you know, two separate forces operated back then."

"You remember their names?"

"Jones," I said.

"Carmody was the other one. Or was it Carmichael?" Jason mused. "I can't remember now, to be honest. Either way, the military police wanted to wash their hands of Melody. We always suspected the man in the back of the car was the baby's father, but we still don't know."

"So…" Hsu looked confused.

"The police and the military police signed off on Christopher. We wanted him to have a good life," I said. "Nobody needed to know about Melody. We don't want people talking and gossiping about him. My parents have officially adopted him and we all raise him."

"But he spends most of his time with you," Hsu said.

I smiled then. "My parents are…a little older. And he's five. They love him…in short bursts."

Hsu nodded. "I think what you all did was wonderful. Say…how did Melody's parents find you?"

"Tinder wrote to them." Jason gave me an exasperated look. "He found their address on the back of an old envelope in a suitcase Melody left behind at Jean's house. They never responded to any of our notes, and now all of a sudden they want to take him back to San Francisco."

"What will you do now?" Oliver asked. He reached out to Christopher, stroking his back. Our son turned and beamed at him.

"We will fight," Jason said. "We will fight them all the way."

Oliver looked at us both. "I want to thank you for your honesty. As far as I'm concerned, nobody needs to know anything. I am still your friend. And, as your friend and as the investigating officer here, I have to caution you to lock your doors and windows. Keep vigilant. Anything I can do, just let me know."

"We will, thank you." Jason walked him to the door. Once we knew Oliver was well out of hearing, Jason turned to me.

"Those people are coming here to Honolulu on Friday."

"Yes, darling. I know."

"They're coming on United Air Lines. This will be the company's first commercial flight to this island. *Ever.* They served the islands with a military contract but they just got the deal to bring passengers." He winced. "I helped them get the financing."

"So this is all your fault then," I joked, putting my hands on my hips.

"Spank me later. This is going to be a pretty big deal, baby. I'm sure the newspaper and radio boys will all be there. It will be like *Lei* Day..." His voice trailed away.

"I had no idea."

"We have two choices, baby. We go meet them and play nice or we disappear."

"We can't disappear." The suggestion shocked me. I could see it all now. The fanfare, the *lei* greetings for the first-ever commercial flight arriving with intrepid passengers from the mainland. We had to go meet them.

Oh, boy. I was dreading it already.

"We should kill them with kindness," I said.

"Yeah. We meet them and then we find out what they *really* want." Jason kissed Christopher's cheek and deposited him on the floor.

"Gecko!" our son shrieked and ran for the wall.

"You think they want something else? What? Money?"

"Maybe. What else is there?"

"They can't take our son," I said.

"Of course not, Tinder."

I loved the ferocity of Jason's tone. "I will call in every favour I have to find out about these people." He shook his head at me. "Your loving heart...Tinder... I know you meant well by contacting them, but as long as I live they can *never* have our child. If somebody cut me open they'd see I bleed two people. You and him."

My eyes filled with tears. I rushed into his arms. "I love you, Jason."

"I love you, too." He kissed me. "You let me handle this my way, okay?"

Really, I had no choice. It had been a huge adjustment taking in the little guy but now we couldn't imagine our lives without him. I trusted Jason completely and knew that if anyone had the means and tenacity to get to the bottom of things it was my man.

"Where is her suitcase?" he suddenly asked.

"In the back bedroom closet," I responded.

Jean had given us access to Melody's things she'd left behind. All we'd found was a gas mask we'd returned to the War Office and a small suitcase with a few of her clothes. When we found her body, I insisted on keeping it. I knew first-hand how it felt to have all tangible memories of your mother erased. Shortly after my own beloved mother died, my father got rid of everything that reminded him of her. He even sold our house, and I'd soon learned he'd been having an affair whilst my mother was dying.

He'd married Linda as quickly as he could and, although she and I hadn't seen eye to eye at all in the beginning, we got along well now.

We'd kept the little suitcase for Christopher, though there wasn't much in it. We'd wanted him to have something of hers when the time came to tell him the truth about his mother.

And so we went to the back room, but, to our horror, the only remainder of Melody's meagre worldly possessions was gone.

"That's it," Jason said. His eyes were icy, deadly little chips in a face set in stone. "Somebody searched this house. They took their time, Tinder. Not a thing is out of place. You and the baby are not safe here if I'm at work. Pack what we'll need for a week. We're going back to Turtle Bay."

"We should report the break-in," I said.

Jason stared at me a moment and slowly nodded. "I need to call Sasumi, and I need to find us a good attorney. Those fools in San Francisco have no idea who the fuck they're dealing with."

* * * *

We packed up the car, and as I kept Christopher busy in the back seat, Jason drove us to the Beretania Street Police Station to file a report. I'd never seen him so agitated but he calmed down once we walked inside. I couldn't help but reflect that the last time I'd been there I'd been arrested for driving Jason's car when I'd given up being a 'working man' by a cop who knew of my history. Jason had come to my rescue, and our relationship and our lives had irrevocably changed.

I stared at the bright, shiny travel posters pinned to the walls. Half-clad ladies in hula skirts strummed ukuleles, their dreamy faces staring up at the moon.

Come to Hawaii!
Waikiki Wants You!
Aloha!
Pan American World Airways: the World's Most Experienced Airline! screamed one poster, making them sound like a bunch of flying hookers. The Honolulu depicted was not one I'd ever really known, and I'd been born and raised here. The images of paradise, however, made a nice change from the propaganda, fear-mongering war posters.

As Christopher scampered around the station now, ingratiating himself with the officers on duty, we filled out the form and answered all the desk sergeant's questions. He was a nice man and said they would step up patrols in our neighbourhood. We didn't tell him we were about to head to the North Shore.

Christopher tugged at my pants.

"Gecko." He held up the tiny blue-green lizard.

"Where did you find that?" I asked. The desk sergeant pointed to the windowpanes on the front door. Jason and I had a heck of a time getting Christopher to give up the lizard but I was afraid he'd hug and squeeze the poor creature to death before we made it to the North Shore. The gecko emitted a series of clicks and squeaks that I'd never heard from one before.

"He has a family here," one of the other officers informed us. "That's how they communicate."

"Your little friend needs to stay with his family," I told my son. "We can't take him away, sweetie."

"Okay, Tinder." He looked so crestfallen that I hugged him all the way to Chinatown, where we stopped to visit the bank. Christopher loved the bank. Come to think of it, there wasn't much in Christopher's world that he didn't adore. Jason paused at Hotel Street. We slowed to a crawl past the now-shuttered hotels that had once featured men lined up for blocks waiting to 'climb the stairs' to frequent the two hundred hookers who'd serviced the military men streaming in and out of the islands. A few were still open but looked even more run-down than they had been when I'd been a resident.

Jason still owned a studio apartment here near the Maunakea marketplace but it was empty now. We hadn't figured out what to do with it. I think he kept it as a kind of safe house in case we ever needed it. It had such sentimental value to us since it was the place where we'd lived together and, of course, where we'd saved Christopher's life.

The banking staff greeted us warmly. We went straight to Sasumi's office. She had been on the verge of leaving the office for the day but Jason had asked her to wait. We all hugged her. Our former baby nanny had come a long way since Jason and I had first met her and given her a home and job. Gone was the subservient, frightened young girl petrified of the future.

She was a smart, formidable businesswoman who was Jason's trusted colleague and my closest female friend. She saw the expressions on our faces and called for her secretary.

"Bao-yu, do you think we have any ice cream in the kitchen for our favourite little visitor?"

"Ice cream!" Christopher perked.

"I think so." Bao-yu, who was extremely shy but sweet and a mathematics genius, took our son's hand and led him out of the office. Jason waited. He didn't trust easily. He didn't trust phones and didn't trust people who hadn't proven themselves to us, but Sasumi knew everything about our lives and was a strong ally. We told her what was going on.

"Why did you write to them?" she asked me, but her expression was doting. "You and your mother issues, Tinder." She shook her head. "What can I do to help you?"

"I want you to run things for a couple of days. I want to keep our family in Turtle Bay. Any problems, you can call me at my father-in-law's house."

"That's perfectly fine. What else?"

"I want you to call…" He hesitated and looked at me. He released a sigh and seemed to sag a little. I reached out a hand and Jason took it, kissing my palm. Sasumi was used to our little displays of affection. She had figured out the private nature of our relationship long ago. She waited—her beautiful, haunting, dark, almond-shaped eyes fixed on Jason's face.

Jason put my hand on his thigh and covered it with his own. He sat up a little straighter in his chair.

"Call The Straw Fan."

Her face paled. "Oh, boss…are you sure?"

He ignored her. His voice became firm. "Call him and tell him I want him to hire his best investigator to find out everything he can about the Hampton family in San Francisco. I also want a tail put on Sooty Maxwell, a low-life—"

"I know who he is, boss. He has an application in with us for a business loan."

My husband grinned. "Does he, now?"

"He doesn't qualify and the whole process was a little…suspicious."

"I'm not surprised. I think he was probably here looking for me." Jason handed her a piece of paper. "This is the Hamptons' address. And I want reports as soon as possible."

He squeezed my hand. "Let's go home, baby."

* * * *

I was worried about Jason hiring The Straw Fan. I didn't know the man personally but knew that he was a local member of the fearsome Triad gang. The Straw Fan was the code name for their liaison guy. Triad members had spread from China, Hong Kong, Europe, and now to the mainland US and the Hawaiian Islands.

Jason always said that in business one should keep one's friends close and enemies closer. I didn't know my man to have any enemies. During the war, his bank — one of the oldest in the islands — gave money and loans to people who wouldn't have been able to get a dime out of Hawaiian-owned banks. Some kept up their payments, some didn't, but he worked with everybody. And no one forgot Jason's kindness.

He still operated the same way. He was generous and encouraging. Chinatown was a thriving business centre and now white businessmen flocked to his bank. Jason helped everybody.

I didn't like to think about him doing business with the Triads but I'd promised to let him do things his way and I knew that Christopher would be the safest child in all the islands. I sat in the back seat with my son, tickling him and playing silly games as Jason drove us to the North Shore.

To say that my father was pleased to see his three favourite vagabonds showing up at his door would be a colossal understatement. Christopher, oblivious to any tension, ran around the house looking for his beach toys. The kid had some stashed in both houses.

"Play with me, Tinder," he said to me.

"I will, sweetie."

Linda came out of the kitchen and hugged us all. "We're so excited to have you back here!"

I sniffed the air appreciatively. "Something smells good."

"Lamb casserole with dumplings and I bought something special for dessert." We followed her into the kitchen and she showed us a package of Hostess CupCakes.

"They're a penny apiece and they're guaranteed to be homemade or you get your money back!"

"Nana. Play with me." Christopher tugged at her dress hem.

"I'll play with you," I said.

"No, Nana." Christopher was tired. Somebody needed a nap. I yawned.

"Poor you. Did you have any sleep at all last night?" she asked, rubbing her hand along my arm.

"Not really, no."

"Why don't you take a nap?" Her gaze included both me and Jason. "We'll look after the baby. I'll wake you when dinner's ready."

"Thanks, Mom," I said.

Her eyes popped out. *Mom*. I had never called her that before. She reached an arm around my shoulders and kissed my cheek.

"Thank you," she whispered.

"Let's go." Jason nudged me. We finished unpacking the car and took everything into our room. We'd sort it out later.

I loved the ocean breeze coming in from Turtle Bay. It was a pristine piece of paradise. My lover joined me at the window.

"Nobody can see us here so we can make love with the blinds up. Should I close the window or can you keep the noise level down while I fuck the hell out of you?"

He made me laugh, but he also made me hard and he knew it. His grin held a predatory gleam as he put his hand to my crotch and rubbed.

I could hear our son's happy laughter outside.

Jason kept the window open but pulled down the blind. Just in case. He attacked me with his mouth. Our kisses soon turned fierce. We kicked off our shoes and socks and everything else went flying, too.

He held me in his arms, his beautiful, tapered fingers holding my ass. I was putty in his hands as his cock sprang out at me. "At least she didn't make jellied chicken for a change," Jason whispered, his expression looking pained.

I burst out laughing. He never, ever complained about *anything*, my man, but I realised now he must have suffered through countless dinners with Linda's favourite post-war recipe.

"You should have mentioned something sooner." I fondled his dear, sweet, beautiful cock. He, too, held mine. "I would have said something to her. Besides, if I never see another radish rose, I'll die a happy man."

"I know, but that's why I didn't. You two are playing together so nicely now." My sweetheart beamed at me. I loved him so much. I wondered why he'd ever chosen me in the beginning. The question was always there and was now as he kissed me. I pulled away and got to my knees. I wanted to show him how much I appreciated being his chosen mate.

"Oh, hell, no," he muttered. He pushed me onto the bed, which was covered in one of Linda's handmade Hawaiian quilts. I wanted Jason too much to think about folding the damned thing back neatly.

"I've been denied your ass all day, baby." He frowned as he got between my legs.

"No. Not denied. Never."

He stared down at me as he ran his hands along my thighs. He leant back and grabbed my ankles, pushing them up. I was almost doubled over on the bed as his mouth clamped down on my ass. I had to force myself not to make any noise. He knew it drove me nuts to have his mouth working on me this way. He sucked and licked until I could feel his tongue entering my hole. His mouth moved over me with such passion it swept me away. He gripped my hips, holding me closer to him. I loved the way he ate me.

"I can't have enough of you," he murmured against me, licking me with long, flat strokes. The sounds he made as he devoured me always turned me on.

It was difficult to reach his cock this way, but I managed it. His hard shaft slid in and out of my fist. I didn't want to let go of him, but I was also desperate to have him inside me.

He moved between my ass, balls and cock, sucking and kissing me. Finally, he topped me off with a kiss to my ass and released me. I knew he needed me and, as soon as he let go of my legs, I allowed them to fall against the quilt.

"You have the loveliest ass I've ever seen," he said. "I dream about it, you know." His hands moved under me, gripping my butt cheeks.

"I dream about your cock being in me. All the time. Fuck me, Jason."

His mouth clamped on mine and his eager cock began to poke at me. I was pretty slicked up from his mouth but it took a couple of minutes for him to get into me. I loved the way he stabbed his cock in hard, then removed it again quickly. In, out, in…oh yes…that felt so good. Out again, in and out—his grin getting bigger as he knew how much I loved it.

He finally stuck it in all the way and I had to cover my mouth with both hands to stifle a shout. The pleasure-pain roared through me, sweet bliss enveloping me as he began to fuck me slow and deep. He usually never hurried when he fucked me, but this was a medicinal fuck as far as I was concerned. He lowered his body to mine and kissed me. I held his ass cheeks, pulling him closer to me, and wound my legs around his.

Jason moaned into my mouth. I could feel us both starting to come. He smiled down at me, my man full of love. My cock rubbed between our crushed-together bellies. He rubbed up and down and back and forth and I lost it completely. I came hard at the same moment I felt him exploding deep within me. I could feel his cock jutting away at my stomach. He came so hard his body quaked on top of me.

For a few moments after we both came, he stayed in me, moving back and forth, in and out, sending sweet torment to my spent cock.

When he finally pulled out of me, he looked down at the mess we'd made all over the quilt.

"She's gonna be mad as hell," he said, making us both laugh.

Chapter Three

I had no idea how Jason did it but, the following afternoon, he got Melody's suitcase back. As my father and I prepared to take Christopher out to paddle a canoe in the ocean, Jason and Linda stood outside and watched us.

We heard a car honking and trotted to the front gate.

A black car waited across the road. Our neighbour's chickens pecked the road dirt kicked up by the car's tyres. We all stood and watched as my husband walked over to the vehicle. The back window lowered. Jason stood for a moment and talked to somebody inside. He reached in. I saw an arm come out, caught a glimpse of a pale brown suit jacket's sleeve and a delicate hand shaking Jason's.

My husband then came away with the little suitcase. The car sped away. I was overjoyed to see that thing. I knew it was silly, but it belonged to Christopher. Jason gave me a satisfied nod and took the luggage into the house.

"Paddle, Tinder." Christopher nudged me. Dad and I returned to the backyard and picked up his canoe. Jason came back to us and kissed me.

"As soon as you return, I have some news."

"Do I want to know now?"

"No, it can wait. I need to make a few calls." He pointed to me and Christopher and looked my father in the eye. "Precious cargo."

My father swallowed. "Yes. I know."

Out on the ocean, Christopher sat between me and Dad. The waves were choppy as we made our way out past the first set of rips. Christopher and I sang the old beach boy canoe paddling song. His lusty voice carried the words out to sea.

"One paddle, two paddle, three paddle, four to take me *home*." For some reason, he always shouted the last word, making Dad and me laugh.

We hadn't been out in the canoe for a couple of weeks. My back muscles protested but I enjoyed the discomfort. Christopher paddled with imaginary oars.

"Paddle!" he shouted. "*Home!*"

Lord, I loved this little boy.

I caught my father's gaze. "Don't worry, son, Jason has things under control." Dad knew me better than anyone.

"You're right, Dad. I just worry." I concentrated on breathing.

"I'm so glad you came home. Linda and I worry about you all in Honolulu."

That made me feel good. I used to think she took my Dad from me...from my mother...which she did. I had also come to realise that caring for my very sick mother had been hard on him. I don't think he could have handled watching her die alone and Linda had been a refuge, a lifeline. So...maybe he wanted to make it up to me, making sure my son and my life partner were safe. And, of course, there was me, too. I think we'd become so much closer and things were lovely between us. He'd been an amazing father when I was growing up. I was one of the lucky ones. My parents adored me, and I them.

Losing that gorgeous woman was the hardest thing I had ever gone through. Losing any of the people I cherished now would be even harder. I tried to imagine my life without Jason and almost fell apart at the mere thought. I knew I would never resort to screwing another man to feel better if Jason were to become ill, but I could no longer judge my father for wanting to…live.

* * * *

Back inside the house, Christopher ran to his father and hugged him, then hurtled to kiss Linda who was sitting right beside him.

Then he ran to the radio and turned it on. He was just like me, always looking for song.

"What are you doing?" I asked Jason, staring at the collection of plastic containers and lids on the coffee table. I recognised it as Tupperware. Linda and I had bought quite a few pieces at Liberty House for our kitchens.

"Linda's come up with an excellent idea. I think we should finance it," Jason said. "Tell him, Mom."

She sparkled as she launched into her idea of importing large quantities of the plastic containers from the mainland and selling them directly to housewives.

"We can encourage them to make small businesses, selling them in turn to other homemakers," she said.

"I heard on the radio a couple of days ago that they passed a labour law in Japan giving Japanese women equal rights in pay and working conditions there. As you know, there are a lot of Japanese women right here on this island.

"I was shocked to hear how many of them want to work, to be productive. But they have no idea how to bring extra money into the home without actually having to take jobs.

"They have husbands who want them in the home. One of my sewing clients told me how depressed she is. She told me there is a Japanese saying."

She paused for a moment, emotion shining in her eyes. I could tell she felt very strongly about this.

"'*Kekkon wa josei no hakaba de oru*' means 'marriage is a woman's grave'. I think this is tragic. Marriage is meant to be the beginning, not the end of a woman's life. And I think this could be the answer. Tensions are still strong for Japanese families. They're having a tough time being accepted even though the war is over. They say the way to a man's heart is through his stomach. I say it's that way with everybody.

"My idea is this. Women can start home-based businesses, just like I did. We can teach them to sell these containers at afternoon tea parties. You'll see— they'll end up being very popular. We'll call them…I don't know, Tupperware parties! What do you think?"

"I think it's a great idea." I studied the containers. "I know they haven't quite caught on yet, but we can show the women all the ways they can store food in their kitchens… We can make tea cakes and let them take some home in the containers—"

Jason's expression turned goopy. "You make the best tea cakes of anyone I know."

"You do!" Linda agreed.

"Absolutely," Dad echoed.

"Sunshine Cake, please!" Christopher hugged my knees. I could take a hint. I busied myself in the kitchen, looking for ingredients. I located everything I needed for a Sunshine Cake, a recipe I'd found in the newspaper the previous spring. I knew it by heart. All I needed were some lemons.

I sent Christopher out into the garden with his bucket. We all kept an eye on him from the kitchen window. As I sifted, stirred and measured, Jason told us that his contacts had confronted the 'beach weasel' Sooty Maxwell, who had indeed been hired by the Hamptons to investigate us.

"They had the wild idea Tinder was his father."

"I *am* his father," I said indignantly.

"No, darling. You know what I mean."

That didn't make me feel much better.

I watched our son jumping for the lowest tree branches as Jason continued.

"He didn't find much except he figured out we're lovers. I'm sure they're scandalised. I don't think we should deny it if they bring it up, but I also think we need to play it down, convince them it has no bearing on our abilities in raising a healthy child. And, of course, he stole Melody's suitcase. He's not a very good private eye. He didn't even know where Melody is buried and we visit her grave every Sunday. Evidently he's been following us for four months."

"Four months!" That shocked me. I'd only been aware of him for a couple of days.

"I think he was largely taking money from the Hamptons and buying himself good liquor until he broke into our house—five days ago, according to him. He lucked out when he found the suitcase. Made himself look like a real hero to Melody's family. Made a big deal of finding the suitcase, only, as you know, there isn't much in it."

Jason looked bitter at the thought.

"It still belongs to Christopher," I said.

My parents nodded their agreement.

"Of course it does." Jason squeezed my arm. "Maxwell now knows he is to stay away from us under threat of prosecution since I've reported his antics to the police." He smiled. I'd never seen such savage glee on my man's face before.

"I made it clear to Dan Liu, the Chief of Police, that my bank won't be financing their annual ball unless they take Maxwell's licence away from him. Guess who's looking for a new job?"

He rocked on his toes looking pretty pleased with himself.

Christopher ran into the kitchen with a beautiful fruit harvest. All his favourite adults applauded his brilliance. He handed his bucket to me and I thanked him for his hard work.

"A mango! Where on earth did you find that?"

Christopher just laughed.

"Do we have mangoes?" Linda asked my dad.

He shrugged. "Guess we do now."

I sliced one of the lemons, squeezing the juice, and grated a little rind into the mix. I poured the batter into the cake pan and thanked God Jason was my friend and not my foe.

Christopher wanted to help so I let him slide the cake into the oven. He slammed the door, making the whole room shake, and tore off to the living room to play with his toys.

"Excellent," Dad said when he was out of earshot. "Breaking into people's houses is stepping over the line. I wonder what kind of work there is for a useless private detective?"

We all laughed. Dad looked at Christopher, busy with his building blocks. "I hate the idea that he was following Tinder and the baby when they went to the beach…a perfectly innocent thing to do. That man is a menace to society."

"I agree," Linda echoed. "If he found the suitcase in the back bedroom closet that means he went through everything…probably all their underwear drawers."

God. I shuddered at the thought.

* * * *

Friday, April 25, 1947
Arbor Day

We all awoke early on Friday morning to the phone ringing. I knew before Jason even raced to the phone that it was one of his contacts with news.

"The Hamptons boarded the flight from San Francisco," Jason reported to us. "They're on their way."

He resumed his phone conversation. Only Christopher was excited that it was Friday morning because his nana had mentioned pancakes the night before, and pancakes we would all get.

Jason jotted down notes as he listened. I handed him a cup of coffee and saw him perk immediately. As Linda and I prepared breakfast, I realised California was two hours ahead of us. Mainland callers never seemed to realise this, but we were getting used to these calls now that Jason was doing more business from home.

I didn't think the news that the Hamptons were on their way was good but Jason tried to keep us all buoyant.

"The Hamptons are not poor," he informed us as we hoed into our stacks of pancakes with sliced mango and coconut syrup. "They won the lottery during a visit to Puerto Rico a few years ago and by all accounts they have saved their money wisely."

"What were they doing in Puerto Rico?" Linda wanted to know.

"They have property there."

Jason glanced at Christopher, who was copying my father by licking every last drop of coconut syrup from his plate. Lord, I hoped my father didn't encourage the child to do such things in front of the Hamptons.

My lover reached for the last slice of bacon. Noticing the longing look on my father's face, he manfully handed it over to him.

"Lloyd Hampton, Melody's father, owns a department store in San Francisco. It's a small business, but he's considering selling out to Butler Brothers," Jason continued. "They want to convert it into one of the franchised Ben Franklin five-and-dime stores. My contacts tell me he is close to signing the deal. He's floated out the story that he and his wife want a short vacation before he decides."

"If he sells out that means he will have tons of my money." My father sounded depressed.

"True, but this isn't necessarily bad news. It means they want something else." Jason's eyes gleamed. Ah, the thrill of the chase. "As a businessman, my job is to figure out what the other guy wants and to give it to him."

"What does she do?" Linda asked. "Is she a lady of leisure?" Her voice dripped with disdain as she asked the question.

"Yes" – Jason nodded – "and no… Molly Hampton has a passionate hobby that might intrigue you."

"Oh?" Linda sounded doubtful.

"She makes her own fruit jams and chutney. By all accounts she spends every season harvesting fruit and making these items for all her friends and family as gifts. Butler Brothers has apparently shown interest in buying some of her more popular jams for franchise."

Linda looked impressed. "She must be a good cook!"

Jason suddenly dipped his face to his plate, licking it so fast that Christopher laughed and laughed, making the milk he was drinking come out of his nose.

"So nice he has someone his own age to play with," Linda joked as she collected the dishes.

Discussing our day's strategy, we decided to keep things as normal as possible until we had to go meet the Hamptons' plane in the afternoon. We'd already made plans for the day before we'd received their telegram. We had no intentions of derailing them.

My parents had really stepped up by sending a telegram to Melody's parents saying that we would all meet them at John Rodgers Airport. They had invited them to stay with us, which none of us wanted, but we were willing to accept having to play host to them.

In spite of the Hamptons providing their phone number, they were impossible to reach. They had also not responded to the telegram, but we'd go meet them anyway.

What we were *not* prepared to do was give them custody of Christopher. We were willing to let them spend time with him and visit him whenever they wanted. Our attorney would draft an agreement whereby we would take our child to the mainland for one major holiday a year.

The whole thing upset me. My biggest fear was that they would snatch our son and abduct him. I was petrified we'd never see him again.

"That is not going to happen," Jason assured me over and over.

I hoped he was right. I got Christopher ready in shorts and a little blue and white Aloha shirt that matched my father's. They both thought they looked spectacular in them. And they did. I loved Linda for making the shirts, which in turn matched a lovely, traditional *holoku* dress she wore.

Tucking a red hibiscus from the garden behind her right ear, she looked every inch the island blossom that she was.

"Let's go," Jason said. He looked as tense as I felt. In honour of Arbor Day, we drove into Honolulu right after breakfast and up to Punahou School, where our son would be starting kindergarten in September. We helped plant new trees on the school's rolling property as part of the big day's celebrations. Christopher loved it.

Punahou's headmaster spoke, saying, "We teach our children here to preserve and nurture the land. We must teach our future generations the stewardship of nature."

We all clapped. I surreptitiously reached down and snatched the wriggly worm my son was trying to eat from his dirty little fingers.

The school teachers all came to greet us, Christopher clutching in his fist an enormous orange the school gardener had given him and all the other kids to distract them from munching on dirt. He didn't want to say goodbye to all his newfound friends, but I was already dreading having to leave our son here on his first day of school. I didn't like the idea of him being away from us for one single second.

We drove to Waikiki and joined the Arbor Day parade on Kalakaua Avenue. Christopher and Jason bought Hawaiian flags for us all. They returned, our little boy on his father's shoulders, waving furiously at the passing Tahitian drummers, the Samoan fire-eaters and the Hawaiian hula dancers.

Some of Chinatown's residents dressed up as dragons as more drummers joined the parade. It was wonderful and festive and had nothing to do with trees, but, like every other Hawaiian lining the street, I loved any excuse for a parade.

"I'm hungry," Dad said as things wound down, so we drove to our favourite Chinese restaurant, Waikiki Lau Yee Chai on Kapiolani Avenue.

Christopher charged through the restaurant like he owned it and darted into the kitchen before we could stop him. He emerged seconds later—a giant prawn cutlet in one hand, the chef's big hand in the other.

"Ah, my favourite family," he said, beaming. "We have a feast for you today!"

He wasn't kidding. The dishes arrived in bamboo steam pots. Chicken, fish, assorted dim sum, vegetables and tiny, bite-size egg tarts—and they didn't stop landing on our starched white tablecloth until we begged them not to bring us another thing. The restaurant was full and we were pleased to see the Hsu family. Little Kimo and Christopher played under our table as we waited for the bill.

"We're having a birthday party for him on Sunday. We'd love it if you could all come," Oliver's wife Kalima told us. She was a lovely mix of Hawaiian and Korean.

"Oh, we would love that," I said.

She and Linda bonded over their mutual passion for Tupperware. I liked the idea of the birthday party. We'd take the Hamptons and they would soon see that Christopher had a wonderful life in the islands with family and friends who cherished him. Surely that alone would change their minds about wanting to take him away?

Jason paid the lunch cheque for both families. So typical of my man. Soon, we had no more excuses and it was time to head to the airport. We stopped at King Street's little cluster of *lei* shops and picked out two beautiful *leis* for Melody's parents. I also selected a third. It was a special one.

"Melody." Christopher looked at me. Tears pricked my eyes as the *lei*-maker wove red roses and fragrant pikake blossoms together. Each and every Sunday we took one to his mother's grave. He knew her name...just not her significance. I let him hold the box the shopkeeper had put it in.

"Mmm..." Christopher put his nose to the lid. "Pikake!"

He knew his island scents well.

Nobody spoke as we neared our unwanted destination. As Jason predicted, people who obviously had nothing better to do with their time had showed up with their Hawaiian and US flags to greet the United Air Lines flight. Christopher, perched on my lap in the back seat, started waving his flag. He broke the silence.

"Oi-plane," he shouted. *Oi-plane* was his version of aeroplane. I corrected him gently, but he said, "I like oi-plane."

We parked outside the terminal. Linda—sitting in front beside Jason, who once again had the wheel—turned to me and Dad.

"I say we all get on a plane and fly to Maui."

She wasn't joking. I was seriously tempted by the idea but I knew my man was a land shark. He wanted to know what our unwanted visitors were up to. Christopher wouldn't leave the *lei* for Melody in the car. He clutched it in his arms, crying vociferously when I tried to coax him to take the other two *leis* instead.

"Melody!" he said, his voice getting louder. "Melody!" he shouted in my face.

I had to let him carry the box and passed the *leis* on to Linda. I was unhappy because I thought it would be a nice gesture for Christopher to give his grandparents their Aloha *leis*.

"Christopher," Jason said in a tone our son knew well. Christopher stopped crying, great streams running from both eyes. He cocked his head, looking up at his father. "Come here." Jason's voice softened a notch. He knelt, taking a handkerchief from his pocket, wiping Christopher's face and urging him to blow his nose.

"Give me the box, darling."

Christopher gave it to him.

"Thank you. Tinder and I want you to give these two *leis*—" He held his hand out for them. Linda complied. "—to the nice people we are going to meet. And I want you to be a very nice boy and say *aloha* to Mr and Mrs Hampton. Can you do that for me, please?"

"Okay, Daddy!"

Christopher hurled himself into Jason's arms, almost crushing the *leis* between them.

"I wish I knew how you did that," I muttered to Jason as we walked towards the terminal. Jason held on to the *lei* box for Melody in one arm. He reached the other around me briefly to squeeze my ass cheek.

"I'll teach you," he said, giving me a wink.

We walked through the terminal outside into the sun where hula dancers and tribal drummers performed. Lots of people lined the gateway that separated those waiting for passengers from the John Rodgers Airport crew who waited to help unload the craft.

The plane loomed into view and touched down. Christopher waved his flag and *leis* madly the whole time we watched the stairs being wheeled out on to the tarmac and people descending the plane.

"What do they look like?" Linda suddenly asked.

"I think she's blonde," I said, recalling how pretty Melody had been. A tall, sandy-haired man stepped tentatively down the somewhat rickety stairs. A brunette air hostess and a pretty blonde woman helped him. He leaned heavily on a cane. I knew who they were immediately. Not only did the blonde look very much like Melody but the man...*oh my God...* He was the spitting image of Christopher.

They made their way towards us. She was dressed in a very formal, entirely unsuitable black wool, long-sleeved skirt suit.

"That's a Charles James suit...the *height* of fashion back in the States," Linda whispered in my ear. She sounded awed. Mrs Hampton wore a black hat, her handbag slung over her wrist. Black pumps and little black and white gloves completed her dignified ensemble.

Her husband, too, wore a black wool suit. I felt like we were all a bunch of country bumpkins in comparison.

To my dismay, newspaper photographers shot photos of the moment little Christopher ran to them, screaming "Aloha!" and trying to lasso them with his *leis*.

People around us laughed, but the Hamptons didn't think it was very cute or funny. They both bent to him, accepting his traditional island offering only after seeing people all around them receiving *leis* from their families.

"Are you injured?" I asked Mr Hampton. I saw that his right foot was bound in bandages.

"Fell down the stairs last night. Can you believe it?" He shook his head. "We thought about cancelling but…"

His gaze lingered on my son.

"Glad you could be here," my father said, stepping into action as the hearty host. "Are you in a lot of pain?"

"Not unless I put pressure on it. The doctor back in America said it's just a bad sprain."

"Well, we'll fix you up in no time! The waters here are wonderfully healing. How was the flight?"

"Long." Talk about stating the obvious.

"How long was it?" My father was still trying to be Mr Congeniality.

"Nine hours. It's good to stretch my legs a little."

"Are you hungry?" my father asked.

The Hamptons ignored him.

"Hello. How do you do?" Molly Hampton's gloved hand touched Linda's bare one very briefly. Her tone was so icy I almost wished I'd brought a sweater.

She flicked a gaze at Christopher, then at her husband. Yes. Their resemblance was uncanny.

When Christopher realised the new arrivals were not very interested in talking to him, he turned to Jason. He reached up for the *lei* box.

"Melody," he said. For the first moment, the Hamptons showed some sign of emotion.

"He knows about her?" Mr Hampton looked shocked.

"Melody!" Christopher said again. He handed the box to Mrs Hampton, who pushed her handbag higher on her arm to take possession of it. She opened it.

"Why it's..." her nose twitched a little. "It's charming."

Charming?

"We thought you might like to visit her grave. We usually go every Sunday but I'm sure she'd enjoy an extra visit. The cemetery is quite close," Linda said. Neither Hampton said a word. They kept staring into the box.

Jason and I exchanged glances.

"She loved roses," Mrs Hampton said, but she didn't show much emotion. She replaced the lid on the box. Jason and I grabbed their suitcases and we walked into the terminal. We passed through to the other side. Jason and Dad spent a few minutes squeezing the luggage into the trunk, then we all squeezed into the car, Mrs Hampton sitting in the front seat next to Jason. My son sat on Linda's knee, unaware of the tight fit for the four adults around him in the back seat.

The silence was awkward, the air humming with questions I suspected the Hamptons were dying to ask but might not have wanted to in front of Christopher.

"I hope you will be staying with us... Did you receive our telegram?" Linda asked, leaning forward to Mrs Hampton.

"We received it." The tone was so chilly she'd have done well selling it as refrigeration. It wasn't really a response. It was frankly rude and I was beginning to really hate their visit.

A thought occurred to me. "How long will you be staying?"

"That is undecided." This from Mr Hampton. Boy, could he be any more pompous?

Jason kept his gaze on the road as he drove up towards the Manoa Valley. I liked Molly Hampton just a little bit better when she noticed with obvious pleasure that the temperature had dropped and that Manoa was a lovely place.

"I love the mist on the mountains here and the trees are so green!"

We parked outside the entrance to the cemetery.

Christopher reached over to me, hand outstretched.

"Candy, Tinder."

"Please," I said to my son, only I realised I didn't have any candy.

"Please," he repeated dutifully.

"There should be some in the glove compartment," Jason said to Mrs Hampton.

She opened it but there was no candy.

Jason caught my gaze in the rear-view mirror. His terror matched my own. It was extremely bad luck to enter Manoa Cemetery without leaving candy at the gates for the ghosts of the dead. We couldn't go in...and if we explained things to the Hamptons they would surely think we were absolutely barmy.

"I have two pieces from the plane," Mrs Hampton suddenly said. "The air hostess gave them out to everybody before we landed to help us stop our ears from getting blocked."

She rummaged through her handbag and produced two peppermints.

"Please," Christopher said. She smiled at him. "Thank you...Mrs." He'd forgotten her last name but he'd shown manners and I was proud of him. Dad opened the car door and got out with him. The Hamptons watched as Christopher left the candy with the stash already beside the big iron gates.

"How...charming," Mrs Hampton said. "Is that for the local...urchins?"

"No," Linda said, "the ghosts."

Mrs Hampton's head whipped around, her expression fearful.

"How...charming," she said again.

She seemed to be having a mad love affair with that word. Dad and Christopher got back into the car. No crack of lightning hit the car so I assumed the old ghosts were happy with their earthly gifts. We drove slowly through, the Hamptons both agog at the bright bunches of flowers and plethora of red and gold papers all over the graves.

"What are they?" Mr Hampton leant forward to ask Jason.

"Paper money," He said, turning to smile at the man. "We just had Ching Ming in the islands."

"Ching Ming?"

"The Chinese version of Halloween...or the day of the dead. We honour our ancestors so they protect us. In the Chinese culture, we burn money for the dead...or a representation of it, so that they have plenty of good fortune on the other side of the veil."

"Do you burn real money?"

"No… Like I said…this is paper money. It's actually made of joss stick paper."

Jason parked off to the side. Christopher was anxious to get out of the car. He loved the graves, especially the ones in the children's section. We always brought candy for the children and I could have smacked myself for forgetting this time. We'd make it up to the babies on Sunday.

As we all walked to Melody's grave, I felt the sense of peace that always came over me here at the Manoa Cemetery. The Chinese truly honoured their dead in a way no other culture I knew did and the place had a lightness of spirit that came, I believed, of the dead appreciating the love still given to them.

The Hamptons enjoyed listening to Jason explain why there was a special children's section.

"Most of them have been dead for over a hundred years. They were the children of slaves…of early plantation workers. Their parents agreed to bury them together so they wouldn't be alone in death."

I knew the story but it still filled me with emotion.

Christopher darted to Melody's grave. He reached for the *lei* box. Mrs Hampton gave it to him.

She gazed down at the flower-strewn memorial for her daughter. I could tell she was taken aback by the flowers we'd planted. The roses and wild orchids. She saw the *leis* we'd left for her and the little mounds of fruit and candy.

"You brought her paper money, too," Mr Hampton said.

Mrs Hampton talked over him. "She's buried with the children?"

As Christopher knelt at the foot of the grave to give Melody her newest floral tribute, she knelt beside him.

She put an arm around him but he got up and ran to Linda, who picked him up and held him.

Mrs Hampton put her gloved hand over the flowers. I could tell she was upset. Had I been her I probably would have been bawling, but she was a stoic one.

"What do you want?" Linda suddenly asked when the woman rose again.

Oh, boy. Talk about coming straight to the point.

Christopher shrugged himself out of Linda's arms and ran towards some of the very old graves. They always intrigued us. Only Jason could read Chinese and would tell us the names of the babies underneath their crumbling, cracked headstones.

The Hamptons exchanged glances. She, apparently, either chose to ignore the obvious reference, or misunderstood it.

"I don't know about you, Lloyd, but I'd like a cup of tea," Mrs Hampton finally said. "It's been a terribly long day."

She marched back towards the car.

Her husband began to lumber after her, but faltered. It must have galled him to have to accept help from my father and me.

Jason ran after Christopher, who'd thought he'd play some hide and seek.

"I'll go after the old battleaxe," Linda whispered in my ear. I almost laughed, but stopped myself.

Jason crossed our path, our son over his right shoulder.

"I found a child," Jason said. "What do you think, Tinder, should we take him home?" His eyes twinkled. Christopher was laughing.

"Yes, I think we should," I said. "He looks...charming."

My dad had to stop walking because he was laughing so hard.

Chapter Four

Mrs Hampton sat on the balcony of the Manoa Hotel sipping tea. She and her husband had booked a room there for three nights. Frankly, I was happy not to have them staying with us, but I was not at all open to their suggestion that Christopher spend the night with them.

We took a page out of the Hampton Book of Rudeness and simply ignored them when they brought it up. Three times.

She sent the hot water for her tea back with the waiters twice. I declined tea after noticing their spiteful glances. I had a notion they might be spitting into it back in the kitchen, but, when she did finally put her lips to her cup, Mrs Hampton proudly proclaimed the tea to be 'quite adequate'.

Boy, oh boy.

Christopher became restless and wanted to play with the water bubbling in the fountain. I accompanied him so he didn't get any bright ideas about jumping in fully clothed. I longed to go home and let him run...take him to the beach...

"He reminds me of his mother."

I turned around. Mr Hampton leaned against a pillar and lit a cigarette.

"Really? I don't remember her being so restless." I smiled at the man. He carelessly tossed his spent match into the lavish, tropical shrubbery. I liked the man even less now. I knew how long and hard the gardeners worked to keep the grounds so lush and lovely. Casual beauty rarely just happens...even in paradise.

"She was restless." Mr Hampton shifted, balancing his cane against his knee. I had the peculiar feeling it had been an afterthought. I wasn't sure there really *was* an injury... He hadn't wanted to come here. But why?

"I know who you are, Tinder," he said. Oh, Lord. If he was going to accuse me of being Christopher's natural father—

"She told us about you. The only male prostitute in Honolulu. I hear you've made something better of yourself since then. But you're still a slut. Just like her."

His words shocked me.

"Apologise."

Oh, God. It was Jason. Christopher, who'd been playing in the fountain, looked at us all. He couldn't have understood the words, but I was grateful when Dad came and took the baby away.

"I'm not apologising." Mr Hampton smirked at the suggestion.

"You're inferring that Tinder is a poor parent because of unfortunate life circumstances a long time ago." Jason moved towards me. His mere physical presence gave me strength and comfort.

"Well, it hardly speaks to his...credibility as a guardian, wouldn't you say?" Mr Hampton dragged deeply on his cigarette. He was enjoying himself. He'd come armed with a trump card, but he didn't know my man. I suspected he had a killer hand himself.

"I don't know..." Jason was so relaxed I was convinced the cards he held were deadly. "I'd rather have a hard-working, honest man for a life partner than a gambling addict with a hard-wired passion for prostitutes who tie him up. Oh, and let's not forget...*Sasha*."

"Sasha?" Mr Hampton's cigarette dropped from his fingers. He swiftly bent and retrieved it, his face sagging. "Who...how?"

"I don't think your wife would really want to know that you've fathered an entire other family in Puerto Rico...do you?"

My involuntary gasp forced Jason to speak louder. "I suggest you quit trying to defame Tinder...unless you want your wife to see the photos I have in my possession from your...er...frolics last night. I know how you really hurt your ankle."

"Shit!" The words escaped the older man's lips, sending his cigarette straight onto his tie. He frantically brushed at it, but he'd started a fire.

In more ways than one. He staggered to the fountain, his walking stick clattering to the ground. He bent over, sticking his chest into the bubbly water. Unfortunately he didn't damage himself, but he would have a helluva time walking through the hotel with his burnt tie and shirt and not drawing some attention to himself.

He stood, gasping for breath, misery evident in his face.

Jason grabbed the man's arm. "You keep our secret and we'll keep yours. She will never see the photos, even though, Mr Hampton, you do look quite fetching in high heels and a pom-pom skirt!"

* * * *

My lover was restless that night. The Hamptons had our telephone number but not our address. Intellectually we knew they couldn't just show up and kidnap Christopher, but emotionally it was what we feared more than anything, and they knew it.

Long after Christopher was asleep, the adults in the house hashed over and reheated the conversation Jason and I had had with Mr Hampton.

"What's a pom-pom dress?" Linda wanted to know.

"Some kind of poufy dress. It's white with polka dots. And his black high heels are to die for." Jason grinned.

"And you have photos?" I asked.

"I will. They're on their way. The courier will bring them to me tomorrow." He paced the room. "I didn't mean to reveal myself so soon but I have an Achilles' heel—Tinder. I couldn't have him insult my man."

"Of course not," my father assured him. "You know, I really dislike the man. Is he…you know…gay or straight?"

"Who knows?" Jason shrugged. He plucked a grape from the bunch on the table. "I believe he's straight but has a fetish for dressing in women's clothes."

"I could make him something to wear." Linda didn't seem to be joking.

"We have to figure out a way to get along with them," Jason said. He checked his watch for the tenth or was it the eleventh time in the last hour. "It's almost ten. I was certain they'd call by now."

Ten seconds later the phone rang. His evil smile returned. Thank God. He let my father take the call then pounced when Dad handed him the receiver.

"Hello?" he said, sounding just as mellow as could be.

There was a long pause and finally he said, "We would be very happy to meet you tomorrow and discuss things. Come to our house in Honolulu at ten o'clock."

He gave him the directions, then glanced at me.

"I'm going to ask Sasumi to watch Christopher in the morning. I don't want him there while we discuss terms."

"Good idea."

My father and I checked the house one last time, ensuring every window and door was locked and that the small booby traps we'd set for any possible intruders were in place.

"All shipshape," Dad said. "I feel like I could sleep for a hundred years." He patted my cheek and went off to bed. I went to the room I shared with Jason and found him lying on the bed staring up at the ceiling — hands under his head in an apparently relaxed mode. I knew the position well. It belied his absolute sexual starvation and as I walked inside he growled.

"Lock the door, Tinder. If I don't get to fuck you right now, I'll go right out of my mind."

I did as he asked. He rose from the bed in one fluid movement and strode towards me.

"You always make me wait," he grumbled, his lips crushing mine. We broke our embrace only to shove a chair up against the door handle. If Christopher awoke and bashed on our door, we'd hear him...but for now, Jason was mine. All mine.

His mouth sought mine again, his hands sliding over my ass, moving my body closer to him.

"When I was on that ship, Tinder..."

I knew the ship he meant. The one where he'd been raped and tortured. It had been a terrible ordeal and his nightmares from it had only subsided in the last year. Before that, he frequently awoke screaming. He didn't remember the episodes afterwards. When he did, they depressed him for days. I had no idea why he wanted to talk about it now.

He cleared his throat. "Tinder...the first time I saw you, I wanted you. The first time we made love, I knew I wanted to do it forever. Does that sound crazy?"

"No. I felt the same way."

He took my face in his hands and kissed me. "I hated the idea of another man touching you. I still do. I never want to think about a life...a day, or a night without you. Passion is finding new and wonderful ways to show your man how much you love him. If I didn't love you deeply, I could never show you my heart. Without my heart, without you, I have nothing."

He took my breath away. Not many men I'd met admitted to monogamy but Jason was proud of it. I rarely glimpsed him eyeing up other men. My feeling was that looking was free, but I'd stopped doing it because I knew it hurt him. His tongue ran across my lips.

"Do you know what I thought about on that ship?" he asked against my mouth.

"No. Tell me."

"I had to get out of there alive because I knew you were waiting for me. I'm so very sorry I went away, Tinder. I'm so…so sorry."

He had apologised to me more than once about taking the mission on board the *Matson* cargo ship. I'd thought I would die when he left but I had also known he was doing it for our country and for his race. He'd wanted to prove his loyalty to Hawaii and to America. He had proved he was a man of integrity and courage.

It seemed to me that we were once again being forced to prove it all over again.

"You're not going anywhere, are you?" I asked, fear seizing me.

"Of course not." His arms tightened around me, his kisses leaving me so breathless I started to get dizzy.

"Please let me suck your cock," I said, keeping my voice low.

"Okay." His smile dazzled me. I got all his clothes off his beautiful body. "I want you naked, too," he insisted. I took everything off fast, crouching to lick the head of his cock, which seemed to leap right into my mouth.

"You have me well trained." Jason chuckled. I sucked on him until his juices started bubbling to the surface, leaking from his perfect glans. I lapped at the pearls that moistened his cock head, then took my mouth away.

"On the bed," I demanded. "All fours."

"You should say 'please'. That's the polite thing to do."

"Fuck you. Do it."

He turned an arched brow at me but he did it. His cock jutted upwards towards his flat, toned belly as he arched his beautiful ass up to me. I ran my hands over his smooth, golden-brown skin. I loved his body and began to lick his tail bone. He moaned.

"Tinder, you do the craziest shit to me and I love it."

"Shut up and take your licking like a man."

He said not a word and, because he was being so good as I kissed and licked his ass, I fed him two fingers. He sucked them like they were little cocks.

I moved my tongue between his ass cheeks. He always acted unsure about my face being anywhere near his ass until I began to lick him. Then he would always begin tossing it around, trying to get my tongue and later my fingers inside him.

It was hard getting my tongue into him but I knew how much he loved it. I dipped in and out of him, trailing my mouth down to his balls, capturing them with my puckered lips. He loved when I drew only the delicate skin of his ball sac into my mouth and pulled on it.

He began to gasp and buck against me.

I pulled my mouth away from his balls and returned to his ass, licking him until I felt he was ready. Gently sliding a single finger into him, I moved around under him to take his bouncing cock into my mouth. He lifted his left leg high to give me more access to him. I sucked until I tasted warm beads of come against my tongue and retreated. He hissed in frustration until I removed my finger from his ass and sucked him again. I put my finger back in, grabbing his balls in my left hand to suck them into my mouth. He groaned when I pulled them back up towards me.

Sliding a second finger into him, his ass closed snugly around them. I reached back around to claim his cock again. Jason fucked my fingers.

"One more," he ground out. I complied. He humped me in an agitated, needy way and I knew he was close. Keeping my fingers inside him, I turned around and lay on my back. He went berserk trying to ride my face. I wouldn't let his cock into my mouth at first, taunting him with kisses and licks. He finally got his cock into me and he reached around, grabbing at my fingers as they sawed in and out of him. He pushed them harder and deeper into him. I felt my pinkie finger joining the crowd inside him. The extra pressure made him lose all control. He straddled my head, fucking my mouth until his cock gushed down into my throat.

His thighs squeezed my head as my mouth clamped down on his marauding cock. He got off my head to lie on top of me. I struggled to swallow everything he'd given me. Jason's face was wet with tears when he slid down my body and sucked me until I came, my orgasm so strong I could hear my heartbeat pounding in my ears.

* * * *

Saturday, April 26, 1947

The following morning, we arrived an hour early at the house on Kuhio Avenue. We all set about tidying it up and airing it out. We'd only been there for a few minutes when the Hamptons arrived.

"That's so weird," Jason said. He and Dad went to the door.

Linda and I had baked a coffee cake in Turtle Bay and we set out plates and forks for it. We put the coffee percolator on the stove as the Hamptons got out of the black car, courtesy of the Moana Hotel. They made fast progress up the walkway, even though he was still hobbling with his cane.

"I really need crutches," he said, easing himself into a chair. "I was just afraid they wouldn't let me on the airplane if they thought I was totally incapacitated."

"Would you like some cake and coffee?" I asked.

"Yes, please," Mrs Hampton said. She was dressed rather formally again in yet another hopelessly warm outfit for the climate.

"Isn't that a woollen dress?" Linda asked her, looking shocked.

"Yes." Mrs Hampton nodded. "I had no idea it was so…tropical here. I have no other clothes."

"Have some coffee and cake, then I'm taking you home with us," Linda said.

"Home?" Mrs Hampton looked appalled. "You mean, you don't live here?"

"Jason and I come here during the week," I said. She was already burning up, I could tell.

"Why not take off your hat and gloves?" I suggested. "You can leave your handbag with them on the sideboard. They're perfectly safe."

"Well, I don't know." She glanced over there as if expecting to see dangerous, wild monsters ready to bite.

"Take them off, Molly." Her husband sounded tired. Linda watched him for a moment.

"Are you in pain?"

"The worst." He shook his head. "I got no sleep last night."

"I have something to help you," I said.

Jason followed me into the bathroom. "What are you getting him?" he asked as I reached into the topmost shelf. "Oh, Tin…not the drops."

"Why not?" We stared at the small bottle of opium drops. Jason had been prescribed them for a kidney stone and said they had made him feel so wonderful he'd wished for another stone.

"Just a drop," I said, "or two."

Jason thought for a moment. "Give him two. He'll be as high as a kite and happy as a pig in wet sand."

We hurried back into the living room. Linda stared at the bottle. She knew what it was.

"Is that opium?" Mr Hampton looked so happy I had a terrible feeling he might kiss me.

"Yes."

He snatched the bottle from my fingers. "God bless you." He opened the bottle, squeezing off a large helping into the eye dropper. He tilted his head back and swallowed enough liquid opium to tranquilise a herd of elephants.

I held out my hand for the bottle but he popped it into his jacket pocket.

"Coffee's ready," Dad announced.

For the next half hour Mr Hampton gradually became more pleasant and sociable. Mrs Hampton even laughed once when my father told a joke. They were friendly and nice, and then the conversation turned to Christopher.

Of course.

"We will fight for custody," she said. "We have the means to do it."

"And we will fight back," my father assured her. "You do realise this was a legal adoption?"

"Not…in an American court," she said, looking less than self-possessed for the first time.

"Absolutely. We are assured by our attorney that our adoption will stand up in any court of law."

She looked a bit surprised. "Can I see the documents?"

Both Hamptons were silent as my father produced the paperwork. He also handed her a copy of our attorney's proposed holiday schedule.

"We can celebrate Christmas here one year, San Francisco the next," Dad said. He and Jason had rehearsed all this a few times. He came off as self-confident and yet sounded willing to accommodate their concerns.

"This surprises me," Mrs Hampton said. "What do you think, Lloyd?" She gazed at her husband but he was in La-La Land. I'd seen him sneaking a few more drops and his eyes were pinned like a big fat cat's.

"I think," he said, his speech slurred, "that I need to lie down." He tottered towards the living room sofa and fell onto it. He banged his foot on the coffee table. When he came to his senses, I was certain he'd be in terrible pain.

He began to snore. Mrs Hampton, however, was dead sober and quite agitated now.

"Why weren't we invited to this...adoption process?" she demanded.

"We tried contacting you," I said. "We tried even after we...Dad and Linda adopted Christopher to reach out to you. I sent you two letters and a Christmas card. I sent you photographs of him. You never responded."

"Why now?" Linda asked her. Jason moved like a panther beside me, taking the chair vacated by her husband.

She glanced over at him and suddenly she seemed frail and vulnerable.

"I...I found out that Melody has another child."

That wasn't news any of us expected. She glanced again at her husband. "She was such a happy little girl." Tears sprang to her eyes. "I don't know where we went wrong. We gave her everything... She wanted for nothing." She began sobbing into her hands. "I can't believe she did this to me!"

Linda took over soothing the woman. She'd really worked herself up into a lather. Dad fetched the cognac from the living room cupboard and eventually the woman calmed down enough to tell us that Melody had fallen in love with the wrong man when she was twenty.

"She disappeared from home and she was never the same when she came back. She fell for an enlisted man, an officer in the Army. She wouldn't even look at another man. You knew her." Her brimming eyes appealed to me. "You knew how pretty she was."

"Yes, she was a beautiful girl," I said.

"But this man... He wouldn't leave her alone. He found her. He came back after her and left her once again. She met... I don't know... She met some woman named Jean...O'Hare, I think."

"O'Hara," I said, getting a bad feeling about all of this.

"That's right. That's her name! O'Hara!" She pounded her fist on the table. "That woman ought to be arrested and locked up! She preyed on innocent girls with big dreams. She came into San Francisco recruiting — that's the word she used, recruiting — women for the war effort in Honolulu. She said servicemen wanted to meet nice women, have a drink, a bit of a laugh..."

Her voice trailed away and she picked up her glass. She saw it was empty. My father quickly refilled it. She sipped. She pulled a slight face as the cognac slid down her throat. She shook her head.

None of us said a word. I knew I remained silent in case she stopped spilling the beans.

Go on, I silently urged her.

She frowned. "Where was I? Oh...yes, well...I thought it sounded very strange. Nice women don't meet men in bars for drinks. Jean seemed like a rough sort to me. Too...I don't know...hard. She was a tough woman."

I thought this was an accurate assessment but I didn't say so.

"She was arrested, you know, for prostitution and she was forced to leave San Francisco. And where does she go? To Honolulu! With my baby!"

Mrs Hampton started to cry again.

"About six months later, Melody came home. She was pregnant. Oh, God...we weren't very nice to her and I do feel quite ashamed of myself. I blame us both for her leaving San Francisco once again... Well, I blame him, too."

"Him?" I was a little confused.

"Christopher's father."

We all stared at her.

"You know who he is," Jason said. It was a statement. Not a question.

"She told me...but I..." She lapsed into silence again. "She said he wanted her to come to Hawaii and she went back. Silly fool." She shook her head. "She was such a fool for love. When she died...well... I didn't want to know about her. But, you see, she has another child, a little girl. Annelise's father is the same man. He gave the little girl to his mother. She died right after the New Year and we have Annelise."

I didn't know what to say.

"She's a lovely little girl. She's seven years old and looks just like Christopher. I... We... We want to protect both children. We don't trust this man. We think he will try and hurt them. He destroyed their mother when he learned about Christopher. He never wanted her…or the babies."

I was sure she was right but he'd left us and Christopher alone. Why did she think he would come after our son now?

"Where is he?" I asked.

She took a deep breath. "He was forced out of active duty in Honolulu in 1942. I guess the military officials have short memories because he's back here. Right after his mother died, he dumped Annelise with us and he moved over here. He's back…and if you care about Christopher at all you'll let us take him and Annelise. We plan to leave San Francisco. You can visit him whenever you want. We're planning to relocate in Puerto Rico."

* * * *

I thought I would never breathe again. Mrs Hampton had refused to say another word and took to our guest bedroom, once inhabited by Sasumi, to nap. Mr Hampton remained on the sofa, though we did try to straighten him out a little.

"He's gonna have a hell of a hangover later," Jason said.

The three of us went outside to discuss what Mrs Hampton had told us.

"If the children's father really is the one who killed Melody then we need to push for his arrest," I said.

"He's in the military. He has some protections," my father responded.

"Not necessarily. He was apparently forced out of here once before."

Jason silenced us all with the words, "He will be made to pay for what he's done, but I'm telling you now… Our child is not going back to the mainland with a druggie and a lush."

"Lush is a bit harsh," Linda said.

"She drank half a bottle of cognac," Dad reminded her.

"I wonder who's looking after the little girl?"

It was a question that concerned us all and one that received no answer until later that day.

Sasumi brought Christopher home. He ran around with Sasumi's kids until she realised that Mrs Hampton was still sleeping off her booze and Mr Hampton was unconscious on the sofa. When he awoke, he would be in no shape for an impromptu party.

"Should I take Christopher with me?" she asked.

None of us wanted her to do that. Christopher had missed us and was crawling all over me, Jason and my parents.

Jason walked her outside and returned with a smile on his face.

He held an envelope in his hands. "My report is in." He shook out the contents and we all stared at the photographs of Mr Hampton in a woman's dress. His female companion looked drunk but attractive. She was a lot younger than his wife, but similar in an ice cream blonde way. Some of the photos showed them arm in arm, kissing and dancing.

"My God, he has better legs than I do," Linda said, making us all laugh.

Jason stashed the package in our bedroom safe and we prepared a late picnic lunch to take to the beach. Jason, Christopher and I changed into our trunks. We left the Hamptons a note letting them know where we were. We walked down to Waikiki Beach, the breeze kissing our faces and, I could tell, brightening everyone's moods.

Linda and Dad sat on a blanket on the sand watching us surf with our baby. Waikiki Willie approached us with a surfboard.

"Pay me next time," he said, waving off Jason's attempts to go back to shore for his wallet.

Neither of the Hamptons had showed up by the time we'd demolished our sandwiches so, in spite of our desire not to spend time with them, we returned the board to Willie and walked back home.

Mrs Hampton was in the kitchen, shoes off, trying to figure out how to work the coffee percolator. I took over as Dad and Jason went to help a groaning Mr Hampton off the sofa.

"My foot hurts worse. How is that possible?"

"You banged it," Jason told him. He and Linda unwrapped the foot, which was swollen and heavily bruised.

"I think we should take him to the doctor," Jason told me. We left Christopher in my parents' care and slid the old man into the back seat of the car. We drove into Chinatown, Mr Hampton drifting in and out of sleep.

"We're always rescuing somebody, aren't we?" my lover asked. His hand reached across the seat for mine. When Mr Hampton awoke himself with his snoring, Jason released me.

"Find us some music, will you, please?" His expression look pained as the train-snore resumed in the back seat.

I found a tune. It was Glenn Miller's *Three Little Fishies*. My hand froze on the dial. Jason braked suddenly. He started moving when the car behind him honked. Never would we forget how often we had heard that song before Pearl Harbor was attacked. Neither would we ever lose the memory of it being the very song heard all over the island when the first bombs had hit.

"You know, I'm thinking we should move." Jason's voice was low.

"Move where?"

"Hong Kong…Shanghai. I don't care."

"We can't move. Christopher starts school in a few months."

"He can go to school in Hong Kong. Besides, until Melody's killer is brought to justice, I don't feel safe about any of us being here."

I shook my head. I loved our island home and didn't want to leave…but home was wherever we went together. If he wanted to move, then we would move.

"Let me think about it, baby," he said, squeezing my hand again.

We parked the car in Chinatown on King Street. We helped Mr Hampton up the stairs to the office of the Chinese doctor who'd helped us so much with Christopher. Dr Dao-Ming was disappointed we hadn't brought our little boy.

"Either he's all grown up or this is somebody new," he joked. He was very patient with the now very grumpy Mr Hampton.

We helped the man into the examination room in spite of a few people in chairs already in the waiting room.

"You were right to bring him here. He's in bad shape." Dr Dao-Ming examined him, urging us to stay. "I might have questions." He poked and prodded Mr Hampton, drew some blood, examined and, in his language, palpated Mr Hampton's foot. The examination went on for about half an hour.

"I don't think X-rays will be necessary. I don't think the foot is broken but he needs to keep all the weight off it. It appears to me he tried to wear tight shoes —"

"High heels," Jason interjected. "He likes to dress up as a woman."

The doctor's brow rose. "Oh. I see." He paused. "I was afraid of that."

"Afraid of what?"

"Excessive opium usage causes hallucinations and other behaviours that are not…typical for a person. I am worried about his addiction. His bottom teeth show a serious relationship with a dream stick."

"A what?" I asked.

"An opium pipe," the doctor said.

Before I could ask more, my lover stepped in.

"He took a lot of the drops from the bottle you gave me last year," Jason said.

Dr Dao-Ming smiled. "Jason, that is not pure opium. It is a syrup I make right here, with a small percentage of the drug. In normal usage it provides the required result — pain relief, some sleepiness. Nothing more. No…his addiction is quite severe. I detect calluses behind his right ear, which indicates he has been lying down on a wooden block to smoke. Only hours and hours of such activity would produce this result."

Jason and I exchanged stunned looks.

"I would like to hospitalise him because he has some heavy congestion in his lungs, especially the left lung. I do want X-rays of that." The doctor frowned. "That has probably come from the opium pipe. He will need professional help for withdrawal, and besides, the nurses there are also better equipped to keep him off his feet for a few days."

He picked up his desk phone. "I'm going to call Queen's Hospital and have an ambulance pick him up. If that's all right with you."

"Sure," Jason said.

The doctor thanked us for bringing in Mr Hampton. "People have no idea how dangerous this drug is." He glanced at his sleeping patient. "An opium death is probably the most gruesome thing a human being can experience. They suffocate because of their blocked lungs. The sensation is of a prolonged drowning…in their own body fluids."

"Oh, my God," Jason said. "I had no idea."

I shook my head. "Neither did I."

We thanked the doctor, who assured us the patient would be fine in his care. "We caught him before the damage was permanent."

I think it was the happiest moment since we'd first opened that terrible telegram.

We waited until we were downstairs before hugging each other. "He's a hop head!" Jason said. "Oh, my God!" He grabbed my face and kissed me right there on the street. "No way will any court of law allow a hop head to take our son away from us!"

As we drove home, we held tightly to one another's hands. We were too happy about the turn of events to say much. Not that we needed to talk. Being with my man, holding his hand, was the biggest luxury and severest addiction in *my* life.

Chapter Five

"I don't believe it," Mrs Hampton said. "He's never tried opium in his life!"

We assured her it was true. We had no reason to lie. She was so upset she called the hospital.

"I want to visit my husband," she told the head nurse of her husband's ward. There was a significant pause. "He's on a respirator? Blackened lungs? What do you mean? What on earth do you mean?"

She shrieked these words, upsetting Christopher, who clung to my legs. I picked him up and carried him outside. I began to climb our favourite tree with him and, a few minutes later, the others came outside. Dad and Jason approached me. My lover stared up into the tree branches.

"I'm going to take her to the hospital to see him. Then I'll get her to check out of the hotel and we're all going home."

"We're not going to stay here?"

He shook his head. "Home, baby. We won't be long."

"Don't go, Daddy." Little Christopher hated Jason to go anywhere without him.

"I'll be right back, sweetheart. I promise." He reached up and kissed our son.

"Look after each other," he said.

Linda looked at me. "I think I should go too. She's a wreck."

Indeed, Mrs Hampton was sitting in the front seat of Jason's car sobbing.

"Okay," I said. Christopher and I would be fine on our own.

"Do you want to head home now?" Jason asked. I knew he didn't want to leave us in the house...not since Sooty Maxwell had broken into it.

"You know, I think it's a good idea. I can get the guest room ready and Christopher and I can start making dinner."

"Yah!" Christopher shouted. "Streetcar, Tinder!"

"We're not going to be that long," Jason protested, but Christopher was excited about the streetcar ride now. Jason dropped us off at the stop outside the Moana Hotel. Within minutes the streetcar arrived. Christopher loved sitting in the seats facing the street and, as usual, sat on my lap, holding on to the metal pole with one hand and waving at passing pedestrians and motorists with the other. It always amazed me how many people smiled back at him.

When I was a child, the streetcar had been pulled by donkeys. My mother had been a strong activist to replace those poor beasts of burden with motorised streetcars. She had told me many donkeys died going up the Pali road when she was a little girl. She'd told me horror stories. Some kids got fairy tales when they were toddlers—I got Waikiki Yesteryear and I thanked God for it now. For some reason, as a parent, the stories came back to me and Christopher listened intently whenever I told him about the old days.

He was happy as he waved and waved, pointing out different types of vehicles and the animals he spotted. Jason and I longed to get him a pony because he loved horses so much. At Punahou School, the children would apparently ride horses, feed other barnyard animals... I could suddenly visualise a future with goats, pigs and chickens running in and out of our house.

"Horsie!" my son shrieked. I wrapped my arms around him and buried my nose in his hair. It smelt like the sun. I knew in that moment I would do anything and everything to protect and preserve his lovely island upbringing.

We arrived on the North Shore a little over an hour later. The streetcar didn't go all the way to my parents' house so we covered the last half-mile on foot. Christopher chased the chickens on the road and petted a cow chomping grass in our neighbour's field. In the driveway of our property, I saw the black car I'd seen a couple of days before.

I paused. At least, I hoped it was the man who'd been to see Jason.

The back door opened and I snatched my son into my arms, ready to run. A tall, thin, Chinese man stepped out of the vehicle.

"Mr Qui sent us to watch over you. I have an envelope for him. Please give it to him."

"Thank you," I said. My whole body shook with fear. I assumed he was telling me the truth. I took the large manila envelope from him and gave him a smile. It wasn't my best smile, but it was all I could muster under the circumstances. He didn't try to touch us as we walked into the house.

Christopher squirreled out of my arms and ran to his pile of toys, and I watched him for a moment. A few seconds later, the phone rang.

"Are you all right?" Jason's voice sounded strained.

"I'm fine."

"Is P'eng there?"

"Who?" I glanced out of the window. "If you mean the tall, skinny man with the envelope, then yes."

"Good. I should have asked him to bring you to the house but I was worried he would frighten you."

"He did do that. The car was waiting when we got here."

"He's a good man... He owes me some favours and I want him there until I get home." There was a pause. "You have the envelope?"

"Yes. I put it on top of the fridge."

"Good."

"Jason, who is he?" I lowered my voice. "Is he... Is he The Straw Fan?"

"No, darling. He's The Red Pole."

The Red Pole. *The Enforcer. Holy heck*!

"Are you still there?"

"I'm here." My voice wobbled.

"Don't worry. He's a nice man with only your protection in mind. If you see them moving around the house, don't worry. I asked them to keep a close eye on you."

"How long are you going to be?" I should have asked how Mr Hampton was faring but, actually, I really didn't care.

"Not very. We're holding off on taking Molly to the hotel for their things. She's had a nasty shock. She had no idea of the extent of her husband's problems and the nurse gave her a sedative. We're heading home now. I miss you."

"I miss you, too." I glanced at our son. "We both miss you."

"Don't cook," he said. "I'll stop by Waikiki Lau Yee Chai and have them rustle up a couple of dishes for us."

"Would they do that?"

"Yes, of course. We'll just carry everything home in the car and return the dishes tomorrow."

"We have plenty of food, darling. Don't buy anything. Don't waste your money."

"It's *our* money and it's only there to be spent on you and Christopher."

"Let me cook, sweetie. I enjoy looking after you."

"Yeah, I know." I could hear the smile in his voice. "I look forward to your...more personal attentions later."

"And you'll get them." I called over to our son. "Come and blow Daddy some kisses."

He dropped his bucket and spade and came running. "I love you, Daddy!" he shouted into the phone as if Jason were calling from the depths of the ocean and couldn't hear him. He blew noisy kisses into the receiver. Jason kissed him back and we ended the call. The sun started to set and I glimpsed two men moving around outside.

The Enforcer. I didn't want to think about what kind of things he did to a person who wasn't under his more...gentle wing.

"You want to help me get dinner started?" I asked Christopher, reaching into the icebox for the chicken I knew was in there.

"Yah!" Christopher dragged one of the kitchen chairs over to the sink and knelt on it. He was the sweetest child, always willing to pitch in, no matter what we were doing. I kissed his head.

"Thank you, Daddy," he said. Sometimes the word slipped out. I no longer corrected him. I was his father and if anybody had a problem with it...well...then, I could always engage the services of The Enforcer. I handed him a bowl of peas to shell. We had a rule. He got to eat one pea out of each pod he shelled. His little fingers began working and I got busy with the chicken.

* * * *

Mrs Hampton—now Molly to all of us except Christopher, who still wanted to call her Mrs—ate very little dinner. She drank two glasses of wine and pushed a few peas around on her plate. I showed her to her room and gave her a fluffy bath towel. Linda lent her a nightgown to wear and ran her a bath but she declined.

"I prefer to bathe in the morning," Molly insisted.

Linda bathed Christopher instead and read one of his bedtime stories to him.

Jason, Dad and I sat in the living room. Jason opened the envelope, keeping his voice low as he said, "This is the man Melody was running around with."

He showed me the picture. I recognised him all right but could have kicked myself. I still didn't know the man's name. He was one of the two military police officers who'd come to our house. Carmody and Jones. They'd asked a lot of questions about Melody.

"Which one is he?" I asked. "Carmody or Jones?"

"You recognise him. Good." Jason's jaw set in a hard line. "His name is neither. Those were fake names they gave us and they're not, nor were they ever, military police."

"No? What are they?"

"They *were* Army officers. Both discharged for raping an island girl back in 1942."

That surprised me.

"They jumped ship before they could be arrested and high-tailed it back to the mainland. The governor of Hawaii is taking a very dim view of open military crimes perpetrated on our people. I think this is part of the reason he is pushing for statehood. It would give the islands extra power under unification. He is aware of this case but unfortunately the statute of limitations has lapsed on the rape charges, which is why this bastard is back."

"He thinks he's beaten the rap," my father said.

Jason tapped the photo. "But there's no statute of limitations on murder. This guy is up on rape charges in San Francisco. He got a ton of money selling his mother's house when she passed on in January. He dumped his daughter with the Hamptons and now he's here again. As far as I'm concerned, we need to get him off the streets before he harms any more women."

"What's his name?" I asked, staggered that such a terrible person could have fathered Christopher.

"Benjamin Spence. I've discovered he is living in Waikiki. He's opened a nightclub. Nobody's seen him for a couple of days, but my informants are searching for him. He's been on island for two months apparently and made himself quite a few enemies."

"We should tell the police about him," I said, longing to check on Christopher in his room. I knew he was safe with his grandmother but still...

"Already done." Dad cut a glance at Jason. "We went to Beretania Police Station before we came home. Molly had a photograph of Benjamin Spence." He flushed guiltily. "Actually, Linda snooped in the woman's purse and found it. Jason recognised him straight away."

"I was waiting for this delivery." Jason pointed to the envelope. "But I felt time was of the essence."

"Absolutely," I agreed. "You said nobody's seen him for a couple of days? Do you think something happened to him?"

My lover shrugged. "Not necessarily. He could be out having fun. The police say he's a bit of a party boy."

I tried to absorb all of this. When I thought back on the visit from Carmody and Jones, they hadn't stayed long. It had been obvious we'd known nothing about Melody's whereabouts. They must have thought we were a couple of saps.

"What are you thinking?" Jason asked me.

I told him and he nodded. "His partner in crime who came to our house with him is also a choice character. He's in prison in Philadelphia on armed robbery charges."

"Not nice people," I commented. I couldn't stand worrying anymore. I walked down the hall to peek into our son's room. He was in Linda's arms, sleeping in his bed. Like Jason and I had done many times, she'd fallen asleep lying beside him. She was holding a large picture book of *The Ugly Duckling*, one of Christopher's favourites. It was about to slip out of her grip. I tiptoed over to take it from her fingers. As I reached down, I glanced out of the window and saw a man peering inside, watching me.

I stifled a scream and ran back out of the room.

"There's a man at the baby's window," I hissed at Jason. As long as I live I will never forget the expression on his face...or my father's. They knocked into each other in their haste to beat each other to the kitchen door. They ran out, yelling at the voyeur. Next thing I knew, there was silence and they returned with a third man. He was Chinese, incredibly handsome by my reckoning, clad head to toe in black.

My cock actually got hard in my pants just looking at him. He had short black hair that seemed to accentuate his rather long ears. He was magnetic. He caught my stare and smiled. Jason caught our mutual gaze and rolled his eyes.

"Sit down," he told the stranger and flashed me an odd look. I finally averted my gaze with difficulty. They began a rapid conversation now in Chinese. I resumed staring at the man. He had an odd elegance I found compelling. I gazed down at his black-stockinged feet and his pointy-toed leather shoes. I'd never seen an outfit quite like it. I was surprised that Jason didn't introduce us but I remained in the living room, my father standing beside me.

"Any idea what they're saying?" he muttered in my ear.

"No." I didn't even recognise the dialect. Jason spoke several Chinese languages but I didn't recognise this one at all. Listening to him speak any foreign tongue was always music to my ears, because before, during and even immediately after the war it had been illegal to speak anything but English in the islands.

Linda came into the room, looking half awake. "What's going on? You almost woke the baby."

"Go back inside," my lover said in English. She looked over at me and my father and turned on her heel. I was dying to know what was going on and I knew my dad was, too.

We were both taken aback by what happened next. Jason and the handsome stranger stood and shook hands. My lover, however, bowed so deeply I thought his lips would touch the floor. The stranger looked pleased. He gave me a wicked glance and left. As he passed the windows outside, I saw two men walking behind him. None of us said a word but a minute later I heard an engine start, saw the sweep of an arc of light, and then the vehicle was gone.

"Dad," Jason said, "can you and Linda watch Christopher for us for a couple of hours. We have somewhere to go."

"Is everything all right?"

"It will be. Can you watch Christopher, please?"

"Of course," Dad said. "Who was he?"

"We'll explain in the morning." Jason gestured to me. "We need to change," he said. In the sanctity of our room, he opened the closet and picked out one of my best suits.

"Wear that, please. Your ass looks lovely in that."

"You can see my ass in this?"

He rolled his eyes. "Funny man. It sits quite snugly, that's all."

I nodded. "Where are we going?"

"To a tea dance. Let's bathe…fast."

He didn't want to discuss this visitor or the tea dance as we washed and dressed. I combed my hair, a strange feeling of excitement in my belly.

"Okay, what's going on?" I asked as soon as we were on the road.

"I told you, we're going to a tea dance." A small smile played on his lips.

"Who was he?"

"The man you couldn't stop staring at?"

I could feel myself blushing.

"You're still the most handsome man alive."

He laughed then. "I'd better be. He's straight…I think. Interesting that he couldn't take his eyes off you, either. What was your impression of him?"

"I don't know…" I was afraid to say what I thought.

"Go on, baby. I really want to know."

"Okay." I tried to find the right words. "He's…I don't know…magnetic. Powerful. There is an unknown quality in his eyes. Almost empty. He seems handsome…but I have a feeling he's a very dangerous man."

"He is." Jason turned the bend at Waimea Beach. In the blackness of the night, I caught glimpses of white and silver sea spray, heard the roar of thunder. I knew there was a storm coming.

"His name is Du Yue-sheng." He glanced at me. "He is the head of the Triad gang in Shanghai…the most feared man in China. He is probably the most dangerous man in the world."

I swallowed. Hard. "What's he doing here?"

Jason paused. "I know I can trust you with this but he is involved with drugs and prostitution… The only problem is that he's become addicted to his own product. People have started to talk and he's in trouble. I'm giving him refuge here in our studio in Chinatown while he is seeking professional help to overcome his weakness. He's a very sick man. He heard about our problem and, to thank me for my help, he has offered his personal servants to find Benjamin Spence."

"Did you take him up on it?"

"Of course I did. I'm not stupid. That's why we're celebrating. I expect Spence to be in manacles by sunrise. Besides, what we're about to experience should be quite special."

We drove into Waikiki. I was so excited I could hardly sit still.

"Ants in your pants?" Jason asked me.

"Hundreds. Where is this tea dance?"

"In a private club."

"A private club!" I couldn't remember ever going to one of those. Since the war had ended we'd visited a few bars and one supper club on my parents' anniversary, but this, I knew, was going to be something quite different.

He pulled off Kuhio Avenue and turned a corner. We stopped outside what looked like a large brown house on Kapiolani Avenue. A Chinese valet appeared out of nowhere. He came to my door and opened it. I stepped out. Jason came to my side of the car and surprised me by putting his arm around me. He rarely touched me in public. He handed the man a folded bill. The man bowed, took the money and ran around to the driver's side. The entire street seemed quiet until we walked up the garden path and reached the front door. Only then did I hear music as it opened and a man in a white dress ushered us inside.

The place was jumping. In the mix of light, music and filmy cigarette smoke I was certain I saw only men in the room.

Jason looked agog as we passed a magician performing on a small stage. "His name is Ah Hing. He's the Chinese Harry Houdini," Jason told me as the man suddenly vanished in a puff of smoke. The audience showed their appreciation, as did we.

Another man dressed as a woman approached us, holding a hostess tray. He was about the prettiest cross-dresser I'd ever seen.

He smiled at us, his makeup perfect. "Good evening, gentlemen. We have mai tais, vicious virgins, zombies, and inside the coconut bowl is a scorpion. I recommend that one. It makes my head spin. What is your pleasure?" He gave me a wild grin. I smiled back as Jason picked up the coconut bowl.

He glanced at me. "Have you ever tried a scorpion, darling?"

I frowned at him. "No. Have you?"

"Not…for a while. It's quite lethal and designed for two. Follow me."

I was speechless and not altogether happy. How the hell did he know his way around here? When had he been here? More to the point, with *whom*?

He led me to another room where the lights were low and couples smooched in red leather booths. They were all men.

My astonishment took over my anger.

"Come sit with me, darling." I felt like I was in some strange movie as Jason pulled me into a booth. He began to kiss me, then held the bowl to my lips. Boy, oh boy. That drink packed a punch. It went right to my head. Lights swirled around the room and people began to dance but we stayed where we were.

Jason started rubbing my cock inside my pants.

"Who did you bring here?" I asked. I thought I might cry.

He stopped rubbing, the expression on his face incredulous. "I came with Sasumi, if you must know." He grinned suddenly. "Are you jealous, Tinder? How exciting!"

"Of course I'm jealous."

He silenced my words with kisses me and kept plying me with the delicious scorpion.

"Let's dance," he suddenly said. It was the furthest thing from my mind, but, as he held me in his arms, I noticed people all over the room in various stages of undress. I couldn't believe what I was seeing. Some of the dancers drifted to several closed dark brown doors scattered around the room. A couple of doors opened, people emerging in disarray, other couples replacing them.

Jason's hold tightened around me.

"Do you like it?"

"When were you here?"

"During the day two months ago."

"With Sasumi?" The music changed to an up-tempo beat but Jason and I remained arm in arm.

"We gave them the financing. Of course she had to see it."

I tried to picture our sweet, little, frightened baby nanny being here. Sasumi wasn't that girl anymore. She was a smart, sassy businesswoman.

"It is a Chinese-owned and operated business. By men, *for* men. Gay men. Ours to use whenever we want. We call it G Bar. What do you think, darling? It's Honolulu's first gay supper club. Very private. Very discreet. Members only. They're importing all the acts from the Forbidden City in San Francisco."

"The Forbidden City...in San Francisco?"

"It's the hottest nightclub in California. Quite...risqué. They have burlesque dancers... Sasumi is trying to have those shows transferred here. Can't wait to see those."

"Neither can I. I feel like I've been living in a bubble being your house husband. My life has become toys and beach balls."

"But I love that," Jason protested, kissing me. "See the singer getting up on the stage?"

I turned my head to get a better look at her as the music stopped. I loved that Jason didn't let go of me even as the others applauded.

She was dazzling. Her coiffed dark hair sparkled — her red, form-fitting dress and matching gloves made her look like an Asian Jezebel.

"That's Toy Yat Mar. She's the Chinese Sophie Tucker." Jason kissed my ear and I turned back to him. "Another drink?" he asked, motioning the waitress across the room. We sat back in our booth, a second coconut replacing the first.

The room darkened as Toy Yat Mar began to sing. I was lost in love, surprised at the turn our evening had taken. Jason picked up my hand and, with an evil grin, led me away from the room.

"But I'm having fun," I protested.

"We're about to have more!"

He led me down the corridor to a red door, outside which a man stood. He opened it as soon as we approached. This section of the house was wild. On the stage at the far end of the room, two men were stripping. The room was sectioned off into low-lying Asian day-beds and small loveseats surrounded by red velvet curtains extending from the ceiling for privacy. Some men had drawn them — others hadn't.

We sat in the first available space we could find. It was a tight fit in the loveseat but it suddenly felt so decadent and sexy to be in public with Jason's arms all over me and not worrying who could see us. The place was smoky but quite seductive.

I was astonished when the two men on stage stripped down completely, one man bending to suck off the other. I blinked in the haze of smoke and flickering candlelight. It was like a scene from the movie *Ali Baba and the Forty Thieves* we'd seen at the Waikiki Theater. The gay version. Jason flipped the tasselled cord on the ropes on his side of the loveseat. I flipped the tassels on my side, releasing the curtains.

We drew them around us for privacy but still with enough room to view the show. In the velvet darkness, Jason reached for my fly and began to unzip me. I was shocked when he bent down and took me out of my underpants and began to suck me off.

Glancing around, I saw that everybody seemed to be getting turned on by the stage performance.

"Fuck me," the man on the stage who was on his knees said to the man still standing. The man on his knees got on all fours and the man behind him mounted him, his face turned to the crowd.

"Should I fuck him?"

"Yes!" they all shouted. I was amazed to find I was one of them. My lover laughed, his fingers reaching under my ass. I kept my gaze on the stage as the two men began to fuck in a state of frenzy.

"Fuck me, Jason." He came off my cock, his fingers stroking at my hole. He fumbled for his pants buttons, unzipped them, then pulled them down. His delicious cock sprang out and I captured it with my lips.

"Hurry," he rasped. I was surprised I could hear him over all the impassioned sounds around the room. I could hear some serious man-on-man action.

Jason pulled me onto his lap. Sweat trickled down my neck as I straddled him, still facing the stage. I moved my ass up and down as he tried to enter me. He kept licking his fingers to moisten my hole and finally got them in. I moved back and forth and up and down until he finally put his cock in me. I rode him like a fuck-hungry cowboy, Jason's hands gripping my body. One hand stroked my cock, the other reached for my nipples under my shirt, taking time to pinch both. He drove me utterly crazy.

We both came noisily as the men on stage moved into the missionary position. We applauded when they came and they took a bow.

Our waitress came in and found us. I was still on Jason's lap, our pants pooled around our feet.

"There you are!" She handed me our drink. "Enjoy!"

If she noticed my cock wedged in Jason's hand, she didn't show it. She walked out again.

"What do you think?" my lover asked into my ear as I sipped our drink.

"I can't think. You just fucked my brains out."

He laughed and pulled my chin down towards him so he could kiss me.

"Did I make a good investment for us, darling?"

I gazed down at him and grinned. His beautiful cock was still twitching in my ass. I liked the place *a lot* but I wanted him to take me home.

"Fuck me all night long," I said.

"With pleasure." He let go of my cock to take the bowl from me. He sipped at it.

"And, Jason, this was an *excellent* investment."

* * * *

Sunday, April 27, 1947

I could hardly walk properly the following morning, but I sure had a big smile on my face. We all got up early, had breakfast and got ready for church. Molly called the hospital. Her husband had been a terrible patient but had been sedated. They suggested she visit after eleven o'clock since he was still asleep.

Linda reminded us we had been invited to the Hsu family's house for little Kimo's birthday celebration. She had made two Aloha shirts for him that would be a family gift. We'd stop by the Waikiki Pharmacy and get him a couple of toy cars to complete the offering, right after we'd visited Mr Hampton in the hospital.

Christopher never minded wearing his Sunday best. He liked church. He knew all the hymns. But I had a sneaking suspicion that what he really liked was the fact that we were going to the pharmacy afterwards.

The church was packed and Molly was uncomfortable in her woollen suit. We returned home after the service concluded so that she could borrow something more climate-appropriate from Linda. Next stop was the hospital. We took flowers and fruit to her husband, who was grumpy and shouted that there was nothing wrong with him.

"They won't give me anything for the pain," he yelled. "They're savages!"

We didn't stay long because the nurse sedated him with morphine.

"Aren't they supposed to be curing him of his addiction?" Dad asked me. What did I know? I looked at Jason, who looked at the nurse.

"Wouldn't you want to shut him up?" he asked.

We went into Waikiki after that and stopped at the pharmacy. Christopher went straight to the toy section and picked up two trucks and a car.

"Mine!" he said, clutching one of the trucks. We all sat at the soda fountain. Molly seemed quite relaxed and certainly seemed a lot more comfortable in Linda's floral creation.

"You look so pretty," I told her sincerely.

"I feel so good," she told me. "I was melting. I think this is the first day I haven't had a headache."

We polished off our ice cream sodas and headed to the Hsu family home.

Kalima Hsu opened the door, her husband rushing right past her.

"You'll never guess," Oliver said, buttoning up his uniform shirt.

"What?" we asked in unison.

"A man just staggered into the police station in Waikiki and said he had a confession to make. He said he was the man who raped Malia Kaluhia back in the war and that he murdered a white woman." Oliver looked astonished. "He said he murdered Melody Hampton. Sorry, but I gotta get to work. They're worried about a riot. The press is there and poor Malia Kaluhia's entire family is there with pickaxes and pitchforks."

He rushed out of the house.

I could hear the sound of sirens in the distance. I could smell smoke. A fire. I wondered how frightened Benjamin Spence could have been…what could have induced him to present himself at the police station like that?

"Come inside," Kalima urged. "This is still a party and we're still going to have fun."

Chapter Six

Nobody listened to the radio with more rapt attention than Molly Hampton as the next hour passed. She wanted to go to the police station to see Benjamin Spence eye to eye but he had already been transferred to an undisclosed location. The small fire started by one of Malia Kaluhia's brothers had been put out, with no charges filed because of the high emotions involved.

The children played and had fun with the party games Kalima had devised. When Oliver returned home, he told us privately that Benjamin Spence was on his way under military command to a hearing for impersonating a military police officer during the war. That, apparently, had been one of his other confessions. It galled all of us that this charge seemed to take preference over murder and rape.

"Oh, no," Oliver assured us. "He had been dishonourably discharged from the Army and therefore they considered him to be their problem. Let's not forget that, less than a month ago, Schofield Barracks had a huge catastrophe on their hands when twelve of their incarcerated soldiers broke out of prison and took a hundred inmates hostage. One of the inmates was killed. He was a local island guy, remember? Three guards are still grievously wounded."

How could we forget? It had been horrific news but since it had taken place in prison the news seemed somehow…surreal.

"What it means is that Spence will be held in a military jail on one of the bases with no hope of escape. They have really buttoned up their security. Once he is tried and convicted, I give him approximately two weeks before he is killed by one of his fellow inmates."

He glanced at Molly. "I am very sorry for your loss, Mrs Hampton. He is a very bad man and I suspect Malia Kaluhia was not his first rape victim. I am sorry he graduated to murdering your daughter. Malia was a lovely girl, too. She was just fifteen. An innocent. Inmates take a dim view of such things."

Molly nodded. "He can never hurt another young woman," she said. "It just seems…so out of character for him to confess. He's never struck me as being with any sort of conscience at all."

"Well…" Oliver hesitated. "He said a friend convinced him it was the right thing to do. I must say he cried a lot. I think he might have been having some sort of breakdown."

Yeah. A night in the hands of Triad enforcers would do that to a man, I was sure.

Molly seemed suddenly lighter of spirit. "I'd like to visit my daughter's grave on the way home, if that's okay?" she asked my father.

"Of course," he said.

When she went outside and sipped her peach lemonade on the *lanai*, I noticed Linda joining her. Good. I was glad they were becoming so chummy. Maybe Linda could convince her not to take our son away from us.

I went outside, watching Christopher and the other children playing in the sun. It was good to see him getting along so well with the others. He and Kimo were a good fit. I noticed my son handing a fallen plumeria flower to a little girl. She beamed at him. *Uh-oh*...he was going to be a little charmer, just like Jason.

My husband came and stood beside me. He still had a big grin on his face from our sex-crazed antics the night before.

"I feel like he is the last piece left in the puzzle," he said, his eyes turning soft as he watched our son playing Pin the Tail on the Donkey. Kalima blindfolded our little cherub, who could not stop laughing. She handed him the pin with the paper tail dangling from it, spun him around and he tottered forward. His hand moved towards the tree where the tail-less donkey picture had been pinned.

He stuck the pin into the donkey's belly. When he removed the blindfold he laughed and laughed.

"Look, Daddy!" he screamed.

"I'm watching," Jason called back.

Christopher thought his tail on the donkey's belly was the funniest thing ever. The kids all took their turns, then came the Battle of the Oranges. The children paired off but our son came charging over to Jason.

"Play with me, Daddy." He pulled Jason's hand and my lover followed him.

The financial ravages of the war had required ingenuity on the part of the island women, whose children still had birthdays in spite of world conflict.

Jason got to his knees opposite our son and took the spoon and orange Kalima handed him. Oliver joined him, partnering with Kimo. The object of the game was for both opponents to balance an orange on the spoon and use this as a 'weapon' to knock off the other player's orange. Jason lost repeatedly. He fell over, pretending to be wounded. Christopher jumped on top of him, then Kimo. Soon all the kids were playing with the two men, who tickled them until Kalima shouted that it was time for ice cream and cake.

In the garden along the wall, she'd set up refreshments. I'm a cake guy, I have to admit. The birthday cake — which Kalima told us was called a Soldier Cake since so many of them had been baked and sent to military base camps during the war — was a rich, moist chocolate cake.

Her whipped chocolate cupcakes were my favourites, though. I demanded the recipe and, as she started to write it down, Oliver received a phone call. Somehow, the hospital staff had tracked us down.

Mr Hampton had evidently emerged from his slumber and escaped his room. He'd found the dispensary and consumed a large quantity of what he must have thought was liquid opium. It had been, in fact, sodium thiopental — a volatile anaesthetic that had brought about the deaths of thirteen patients treated at Tripler Army Hospital immediately after the attack on Pearl Harbor.

He was in respiratory failure and his vital organs were shutting down fast.

"The nurse said he's suffered a massive overdose. She said she has no idea how he's even still alive," Molly told us, her hand shaking as she held the receiver.

We left Christopher in Kalima's care and drove to the hospital, with Oliver at the wheel of his car. It was a tight squeeze but I think Molly appreciated the fact that we all jumped to her rescue.

By the time we arrived at Queen's Hospital, Mr Hampton had died.

* * * *

Tuesday, April 29, 1947

Jason arranged with the Honolulu City Council for Lloyd Hampton to be buried beside his daughter at the Manoa Chinese Cemetery. For a couple of crazy days, the bereft widow talked about exhuming her daughter and having both of her loved ones interred in San Francisco. When council officials refused to even consider the request, she became resigned to both of them being buried in Hawaii.

"I don't know what to do with myself," she said. She cried off and on and wafted around the house in Turtle Bay, which she seemed to like more than the house on Kuhio Street. She liked picking fruit in the garden and started making her first jam, encouraged by Linda who'd said, "Doing something will shake her out of the doldrums."

Molly seemed grateful when Jason and I took over the funeral plans. Christopher spent the morning of the service with Oliver's family. Our tiny son had plenty of time to learn about death. Once again, we were at the Manoa Cemetery for a very small, final goodbye. As rain splashed from the sky and a rainbow arced in the distance, I felt Melody was waiting for her dad. Knowing that sweet-hearted girl, she would forgive her old man his earthly sins.

Now Molly turned and stared at the rainbow as the sun poked through the gloomy clouds.

"That is a very good sign," my father told her. "It means Heaven is waiting for him."

Molly sobbed into her handkerchief. She left a *maille lei* on the dirt mound for her husband and a fresh, extra thick rose and pikake *lei* for Melody.

"We got him, darling," I heard her say as she put her hand on the foot of the grave. She stood, yanking down her jacket, her eyes bright with tears. She'd donned her woollen suit for the occasion and suffered through a long ride back to Turtle Bay in it.

We had retrieved her luggage from the hotel a few days before but she had barely opened it. "I can't stand to look at it," she'd apparently told Linda when she'd offered to help her unpack.

As soon as we returned from the funeral, she put on one of her new island sun frocks and told us she wanted to stay a while.

"Of course," Linda said. She looked as relieved as I felt that she wasn't planning to hightail it back to California.

"I'm thinking I should go home and get Annelise. She should know her brother." She seemed to sag a little. "I do hate flying, though…and my sister who is looking after her is petrified to set foot on board a plane."

Jason immediately offered a perfect solution. "My assistant, Sasumi, can have her sister in San Francisco bring Annelise here. Sasumi has longed to bring her sister here. How would you feel about that?"

"Why...I would love that. You know...I've been thinking. It's about time I made some chutney. I think I'll pick some peaches." She wandered off to the garden, Christopher running after her with the fruit bucket in his hands.

"See, darling," my lover said putting his arm around me and kissing me, "the jigsaw is almost completed."

* * * *

Monday, May 5, 1947

We were all excited about Annelise arriving in the afternoon with Sasumi's younger sister, Lian.

Now, however, it meant we needed more space.

During the war, I had designed my parents' house and another one on a neighbouring property that had been intended to be our home—mine, Jason's and Christopher's. However, we'd grown quite complacent with the house on Kuhio Avenue and it was frankly more convenient to stay there since Jason worked five minutes away in Chinatown. So, we had rented out our finished property, never having been inside it.

Our tenants had given notice a couple of days before and Jason, Christopher and I went to view the house. My fantasies of it being move-in ready were just that—our dream house was in deplorable shape. The hardwood floors were a disaster. The walls needed painting, windows were broken and there was a weird smell that turned out to be a dead mongoose under the house.

"We can fix it up," Jason said, looking depressed. The house wouldn't be ready for our guests, but we'd deal with it.

"Lian, the kids and us...we'll all stay in the house on Kuhio," Jason said. When we made this announcement to Linda, she was upset.

"Hell, no," she said. "Take that bossy bitch Molly with you. She makes passes at your father."

"She does?" This surprised me. How come I hadn't noticed?

Molly didn't particularly want to leave the North Shore, so I showed her the house we planned to move to once it was in better shape. She loved it.

"How long will it take to fix up and what in God's name is that foul odour?"

Jason called in some favours and organised a cleaning and painting crew that very day. By the time we got ready to go pick up our new arrivals, I noticed the big smile on Linda's face as she and Dad drove in their own car. I could tell she liked having my father back to herself.

At the airport, we met Sasumi and her family. Sasumi — our hard-nosed little business woman — crushed me into her arms and hugged me, weeping on my neck. "Thank you for flying my sister here," she said. "I bet she's wearing a kimono when she gets off the plane, poor, downtrodden little thing."

I patted her on the back, wondering how long it would take Linda to get Lian into modern clothing. We stood waiting, Christopher clutching the flower *leis* for our guests. He waved like mad at the plane descending towards us. It was a thrilling moment to see the landing gear of the Pan American flight opening up and the pilot making such a soft landing on the tarmac.

"What kind of plane is it, Christopher?" Jason asked our son over the noise.

Christopher stopped waving to look up at his father. "It's a DC 4, Daddy!"

He resumed waving. As soon as we saw a pretty Chinese girl—as predicted, in ceremonial garb—leading a little blonde-haired darling down the stairs, we all knew it was them.

"Is that her? Is that my sister, Daddy?" Christopher hopped up and down in excitement. He charged across the tarmac, right under a ground attendant's arm, falling flat on his face. He got up quickly and ran, flowers falling off one of his *leis*. The two children ran to each other and embraced. It brought tears to my eyes. Christopher completely ignored Lian, who held out her arms to him.

He grabbed Annelise's hand and raced back to us. "She's here, Daddy! She's here!"

We all took turns hugging Annelise. Then we took the two visitors to Waikiki Lau Yee Chai—fast becoming our family's home of celebration…not including the private celebrations I hoped to keep sharing at G Bar with Jason.

* * * *

Annelise was a sweet little girl who had clearly missed Molly. She never asked her grandmother about Lloyd, though, which surprised me.

"I'll tell you the truth," Molly told me much later. "Annelise was always a little afraid of him. He used to come home in such terrible moods and I couldn't understand why. Now I know why and I feel so angry. I'm so stupid."

"No, you're not," I said.

"Yes, I am. How could I not seen he was a druggie? He used to have terrible breath and could never sleep. In the last few weeks he had a very bad cough but refused to get help."

She gripped my arm. "Please don't tell anybody but I used to find my underwear…slips and such…all stretched out and my best shoes scuffed. I caught him dressed in my clothes once. Does that mean he was, you know…homosexual?"

This was the closest she and I had ever come to discussing my sexuality. I assured her that cross-dressing was no indication of her husband being gay.

"Many straight men enjoy dressing as women."

"How do their wives put up with it?" She shuddered. "I had to start hiding my best shoes because he didn't look after them."

That was as far as our discussion went. But that night, as Jason and I tucked the kids into their matching beds—separated by bedside tables with a blue lamp for Christopher and a pink one for Annelise—my biggest wish was that Molly and Annelise would stay with us. Forever. It takes a village to raise a child, and, in Hawaii, it is our fondest, best-inherited practice from the ancients.

Annelise was *ohana*—our family now. I read to the children, hoping it would be the first of many, countless nights I'd get to watch them drifting off to sleep.

I raced to our bedroom hoping for some moon-time frolics with my man but he was already asleep. The past few days had really worn him out. I snuggled beside him, wrapping myself around his warm body. I put my palm on his bare chest and felt his heartbeat. It was the most beautiful sound in the whole, wide world.

* * * *

Tuesday, May 6, 1947

When the kids banged on our bedroom door at five a.m. ready for action, for one brief moment I second-guessed myself. Did I want this mayhem every day?

Yes, I did.

My lover stirred. "I owe you a hot fuck," he said.

"I'll meet you in the bathroom in ten minutes," I promised.

He kissed me. "I'm timing you, baby."

With Benjamin Spence in custody, Jason was returning to his first full day of work that morning. We would be resuming our normal routine. The beach for me and Christopher—and now, Annelise—the world of high finance for Jason.

Molly wanted to come with us and that was fine by me.

With the kids safely occupied eating pancakes and bacon under Molly's watchful eye, I raced to the bathroom.

Jason was already in the bathtub. His cock bobbed to the surface of the steaming water.

"Ah, my favourite concubine," he purred as I locked the door.

"I'd better be your *only* concubine, mister," I said, showing him a fist.

"You just made my cock hard." Jason grinned lazily at me. He was a man of his word. His gorgeous shaft was rigid and flying high, straight up. Well, this was a nice way to start the day.

I shucked off my pyjamas and knelt beside the tub. I kissed him and bent my head to suck him into my mouth.

"Fuck!" His ass rose from the water. "I have no idea why hot water really revs my engine," he said, "but you need to get right on top of me, now."

He reached behind his head for a tube of K-Y Jelly. He rubbed some of it onto my ass. It worked until I got too close to the water but I didn't care. I needed my man inside me. I rode him hard and fast, bouncing up and down on his hard cock as Jason took turns teasing my nipples with his tongue.

Water sloshed everywhere but I didn't care. We fucked like demented bunnies, his tongue in my mouth and my cock in his possessive grip as we both came.

"Sorry about the clean-up," he whispered into my mouth. I wasn't. My butt was on fire in the best possible way. He drained the tub and helped me dry the floor. As I piled up the used towels to throw into the washing machine, Jason got dressed.

I went to check on the children and almost had a heart attack. Their uneaten breakfasts were still on the plates. The kitchen door was open. They were all gone.

"Jason!" I screamed. He came running in his underpants and shirt.

"What the..." His face went pale. "We have to get dressed. Come on, babe, they can't be far."

We threw on some things and ran back to the kitchen and out of the back door. Our car was in the driveway so she hadn't taken that. We went berserk running up and down the street screaming for Christopher, Molly and Annelise. I would kill her. When I found the woman I would totally strangle her.

Back at the house, Jason called the police whilst I had a panic attack against the kitchen sink. Suddenly, I saw them coming along the footpath.

"They're back!" I shouted.

"Never mind!" Jason screamed into the phone and dropped the receiver. We ran outside, both of us hysterical. Christopher and Annelise were skipping along holding hands. Molly was holding a cake.

"Goodness," she said, looking shocked. "What's the matter? What happened?"

I grabbed Christopher, Jason grabbed Annelise, and we pulled them into our arms.

"It's okay, Daddy," Christopher said as I kissed his little face over and over.

"Were you worried about us?" Molly really seemed surprised. "We just went next door. I bartered my first jams. Linda said it's the old Hawaiian way. Look, they baked us a cake...it's called a Red Velvet Cake. Isn't it a thing of beauty?"

I wanted to drop-kick the damned plate into the middle of the street but it would have to wait for when we were alone.

Judging by our tears and apparent trauma, she knew she'd made a mistake.

"I should have left a note," she said, looking genuinely contrite. "I thought we'd only be a few minutes."

"A lot can happen in a few minutes," Jason told her. "Just leave a note next time." I knew he hated leaving me and the kids but he had to get to work.

"Bring everyone to Chinatown for lunch," he said. "We'll open a bank account for Annelise."

"Just one thing," Molly said. "I've been thinking... I really want to stay but I have to make a decision about the store Lloyd and I own in San Francisco. We've had a very good offer to sell. I think it's worth more. Would you be willing to handle the sale for me?" she asked Jason.

Of course, he pretended to know nothing about it.

"You can count on me," he said.

He hugged us all goodbye. Christopher and I were bereft as we waved goodbye to him.

Our little boy started to cry. Jason braked the car in the driveway and ran back to us for another hug.

"I'm going to see you both in a few short hours," he said, tears brimming in his own eyes. The thought of Christopher being gone still upset him, I could tell. "I'm going to see you both..." he hesitated, looking into my eyes, "lickety-split."

He knew the significance of the word. It was part of our history. Part of the way we'd met. It was a promise of forever, a future with no separations.

My mouth crushed his in a giant kiss and he ran back to the car again.

Christopher reached up into my arms and I held him. Tight.

"Daddy," he asked after the longest time, "how long is lickety-split?"

"It's not long," I told him, tears falling down my face. I just couldn't stop them. "Lickety-split is very fast."

"Good," he said, his little hand on my face. "Because I miss Daddy already."

"So do I, sweetie." I took a deep breath and kissed his nose. "But first, I think you and I have a date with Waikiki."

I put him on the ground.

"Yay!" he screamed. "Annelise. We're going to the beach!"

Inside the house, the kitchen smelt of bacon, love, and peach jam on the stove.

I hugged Molly as she stirred her pot.

"Goodness," she said, "what was that for?"

"For not taking our son away from us."

She smiled at me. It was a dazzling smile. "I couldn't take what isn't mine, Tinder. Not in a million years."

The children ran around the house, making more mess and noise than two children ought.

"Can I play some music, Daddy?" Christopher asked, turning on the big old radio in the living room.

Why was I not surprised when the song that came on was *Three Little Fishies*? It was always there…just when I needed it most.

Sunshine Cake

Ingredients:
1 cup sifted cake flour
½ teaspoon salt
5 egg yolks, beaten
7 egg whites, beaten
1 teaspoon cream of tartar
1 ¼ cups sugar
1 teaspoon any desired flavoring

Directions:
Sift the flour once, measure and resift twice with the salt. Beat the egg yolks until thick and lemon-coloured. Beat the egg whites until foamy, add the cream of tartar and beat until stiff, but not dry. Add the sugar gradually and beat until the mixture holds in soft peaks. Fold in the beaten egg yolks and flavouring. Fold in the flour gently but thoroughly to avoid breaking air cells in the egg mixture. Pour the batter into an ungreased 10-inch tube pan and bake in a moderate oven, 350 degrees F, for about 50 minutes, or until done. Remove from oven and invert for 1 hour, or until cool. When cool, frost with a thin coating of confectioners' sugar, or sprinkle with sifted confectioners' sugar.

— Created by Mrs Mary Martensen, 1946

Chocolate Whipped Cream Cupcakes

Ingredients:
½ cup shortening

1 cup sugar

2 eggs

2 squares unsweetened chocolate

2 cups sifted flour

1 teaspoon soda

½ teaspoon salt

1 cup buttermilk or soured milk (add 1 teaspoon lemon juice and set aside for 1 hour)

1 teaspoon vanilla

Directions:

Cream the shortening, add sugar, and cream together until light and fluffy. Add the eggs, one at a time, beating well after each addition. Add the chocolate, which has been melted and cooled, and blend well.

Sift the flour once, measure and resift twice with the soda and salt. Add to the batter alternately with the buttermilk, beating until smooth after each addition. Add vanilla. Fill twelve cupcake pans, which have been greased, two-thirds full with the batter. Bake in a 350-degree oven for about 20 minutes, or until done.

When cupcakes are cool, with a small, sharp, pointed knife cut a cone-shape from the top of each. Remove and fill hollowed-out portion with slightly sweetened whipped cream. If desired, a larger hollow can be made in the cupcake. Also, ice cream can be used in place of whipped cream to fill the hollow centers. Place top (which was removed from cupcake) on top of whipped cream and pour chocolate sauce over the top.

To make the chocolate sauce:

Combine in a saucepan 1 square unsweetened chocolate, cut in pieces, 1 cup sugar, 2 tablespoons corn syrup, 1 tablespoon butter and one-third cup hot water. Blend well and cook over low heat, stirring constantly until mixture comes to boiling point, then cook for 5 minutes. Cool slightly and add a few grains of salt and ½ teaspoon vanilla. Serve warm or cold.

— From Mrs Mary Martensen, 1946

Soldier's Cake

Ingredients:
  2 cups sifted cake flour
  1 teaspoon baking soda
  ¼ teaspoon salt
  1 ½ squares unsweetened chocolate
  ½ cup margarine
  1 ½ cups sugar
  2 eggs, beaten
  1 teaspoon vanilla
  ½ cup buttermilk
  ½ cup water

Directions:
Sift together flour, soda and salt. Melt chocolate over hot water; cool. Cream margarine until soft, light and fluffy. Add beaten eggs and beat mixture until smooth. Stir in vanilla and cooled chocolate. Combine buttermilk and water. Add alternately with sifted flour to the creamed margarine mixture, beginning and ending with flour and beating until smooth after each addition. Line two 8-inch cake pans with wax paper and grease the sides; fill with batter. Bake in a moderate oven, 350 degrees F, for 27 to 30 minutes. Turn out onto cake racks and cool. When cool, spread with any desired frosting. Makes two 8-inch layers.

The Brownsville Herald — Brownsville, Texas, 1942

Simple Remedy For 'Runny' Icing Takes the Cake

To keep frosting from running down over the sides of the cake when you want to ice just the top, try fastening a double band of heavy waxed paper around the cake with toothpicks, having the paper extend up over the edges sufficiently high to hold the frosting easily, before icing is spread. Do not remove paper until frosting is sufficiently cooled and hard.

The Brownsville Herald — Brownsville, Texas
September 16, 1942

About the Author

A.J. Llewellyn lives in California, but dreams of living in Hawaii. Frequent trips to all the islands, bags of Kona coffee in the fridge and a healthy collection of Hawaiian records keep this writer refueled.

A.J. never lacks inspiration for male/male erotic romances and on the rare occasions this happens, pursues other passions such as collecting books on Hawaiiana, surfing and spending time with friends and animal companions.

A.J. Llewellyn believes that love is a song best sung out loud.

A.J. Llewellyn loves to hear from readers. You can find her contact information, website details and author profile page at http://www.total-e-bound.com.

Total-E-Bound Publishing

www.total-e-bound.com

Take a look at our exciting range of literagasmic™
erotic romance titles and discover pure quality
at Total-E-Bound.